JFK

KILGALLEN

OBAMA

&

THE NEW WORLD

ORDER

JFK – Kilgallen – Obama
&
The New World Order

by
Dan McQuade
© 2011

First published 2011
by Stagedoor Publishing
London WC1N 3XX UK

www.zoism.co.uk

ISBN 978-0-9521620-8-7

This book is dedicated to the memory of President John F. Kennedy and to all those innocent souls who died as a direct result of his assassination.

Photographs

Grateful acknowledgement for the use of photos to:

The Johnnie Ray Collection for the pictures of Johnnie Ray.
The Billy Rose Collection, The Lincoln Centre, for the pictures of Dorothy Kilgallen.

Most of the remaining are in the public domain and out of copyright. For the two that are not we have tried to trace ownership without success but fully acknowledge relevant copyright ownership.

Front Cover Picture

A Light Extinguished
By
Mike Shaw

This painting was started in early 1963 for a customer in New York, it's title then was *A Shining Light*. When the shock news of JFK's death was announced Mike changed it to *A Light Extinguished.*

The painting was completed in January 1964 and has changed hands several times over the years, and moved around the World. At present it is in a private collection in the UK.

'For in the final analysis our most basic common link, is that we all inhabit this small planet, we all breath the same air, we all cherish our children's future, we are all mortal.'

- JFK speech at American University, Washington DC, June 10th 1963

'The Chinese use two brush strokes to write the word "Crisis". One brush stroke stands for danger; the other for opportunity. In crisis be aware of danger – but recognize the opportunity.'

- JFK speech in Indianapolis, April 12th 1959

'A constitution of Government once changed from freedom can never be restored. Liberty once lost is lost forever.'

- John Adams, 2nd President of the United Stated of America

'The great masses of the people will more easily fall victim to a great lie than to a small one.'

- Adolf Hitler (Mein Kampf)

'Everything pertaining to what's happening has never come to the surface. The World will never know the true facts, of what occurred, or my motives. The people who had so much to gain and had such ulterior motives for putting me in the position I'm in, will never let the true facts come above board to the World.'

- Jack Ruby making a statement to the press after he has been allowed a new trial

'Well, you won't see me again. I tell you that a whole new form of Government is going to take over the country, and I know I won't live to see you another time.

Gentlemen, I want to tell the truth, but I cannot tell it here. If you want a fair shake out of me, you have to take me to Washington.'

- Jack Ruby, in fear of his life, talking to the Warren Commission

'There is nothing we can do at this point, because we are facing a formidable and dangerous enemy and we no longer control the Government. But I swear, we will know what happened in Dallas, and justice will be done when the Kennedys regain the White House.'

- Robert Kennedy speaking at the grief-stricken family gathering at the White House in preparation for the President's funeral. Quoted by British born film actor Peter Lawford, brother-in-law to JFK (married to Patricia Kennedy).

This is a small section of a speech made by President John F. Kennedy in 1961. In it he tries to warn the people about powerful secret societies at large in America, and the Western World:

'The very word "secrecy" is repugnant in a free and open society; and we are as people inherently and historically opposed to secret societies, to secret oaths and secret proceedings. We decided long ago that the dangers of excessive and unwarranted concealment of pertinent facts far outweighed the dangers which are cited to justify it. Even today, there is little value in opposing the threat of a closed society by imitating its arbitrary restrictions. Even today there is little value in insuring the survival of our nation if our traditions do not survive with it. And the is a very grave danger that an announced need for increased security will be seized upon by those anxious to expand its meaning to the very limits of official censorship and concealment. I do not intend to permit this to the extent that it is in my control. And no official of my administration, whether his rank is high or low, civilian or military, should interpret my words here tonight as an excuse to censor the news, to stifle dissent, to cover up our mistakes or to withhold from the press and the public the facts they deserve and have a right to know.'

'For we are opposed by a ruthless conspiracy that relies on covert means for expanding its sphere of influence on infiltration instead of invasion, on subversion instead of elections, on intimidation instead of free choice, on guerrillas by night instead of armies by day. It is a system which has conscripted vast human and material resources into the building of a tightly knit, highly efficient machine that combines military, diplomatic, intelligence, scientific, and political operations.'

Chapter 1 – Mickey, Della, Bob and Zian

My mobile on the dash signalled a call. I pressed the speakerphone, 'Dan McQuade speaking.'

'Where the hell are you, Daniel?' It was Bob's voice. Bob, Robert Appleby runs Stagedoor Publishing. He's beaten off those debt collecting wolves that gather at my door with monotonous frequency many times lately.

'I'm in heavy traffic crawling up Regent Street on my way home. I have Della with me,' I added that in case he said something I'd rather she didn't know.

'Sounds like you're driving a high powered sewing machine.'

'Don't knock the hat.' (Daihatsu sports car) 'This tiny 600cc engine took me up to 110 mph on the motorway coming into town, plus I have the top down and Ry Cooder on the stereo. Call round this evening. I'll be home in 20 minutes.'

'I shall do Daniel, because I can't stand any more of that dreadful noise, goodbye.' I've told him to call me Dan but he insists on Daniel. He's told me to address him as Robert but I insist on Bob, just to annoy the lovable old snob.

My home is a small, and some say grubby, flat in North Soho. Della, my partner, lives there with me, well off and on. She was a stripper in one of the clip joints over in Dean Street but now she tells me she's an erotic pole dancer, so when she gets a booking she just takes off for a couple of days or maybe weeks. Like me she was born in London but is of West Indian descent so she likes loud music and partying, sometimes I find it hard to keep up with her.

My other companion is Mickey; a blue Hyacinth Macaw. That's the largest of all Macaws at nearly 4ft tall and a wing span of over 4ft. He hails from Brazil, and when he's in one of his screeching moods the people on the other side of London can hear him. I won't cage a bird, although he has a large one that he goes into at night but during the day he's got the whole flat to fly around. I would describe him as silly tame, liking nothing better than to sit on my shoulder as I move around. About four years back a guy owed me a grand. He couldn't pay. I was thinking about giving him a severe slapping when he asked if I'd like Mickey instead of the money; he didn't want him anymore and he was in a tiny cage 24/7. So I took him on. Best move I ever made. We've been pals ever since. OK so I'm nuts about animals. Well we all have our problems.

The Soho area of London is known for vice, prostitutes, drugs, clubs, pubs, gangsters, and various assorted weirdos. I've lived here most of my life; anything goes in its seven miles of tiny backstreets. But if you cross Oxford

Street you enter Fitzrovia, better known as North Soho. It's more low key, quieter, except for Mickey of course. You get away from the non-stop noise of Soho's late night clubbers, and police sirens.

I'd taken a shower and just grabbed a sandwich when Bob rang the intercom. I told Della to pour three Sherries. He always looked as though he'd come straight from Savile Row; immaculately dressed and business like in manner. I like the guy. Della can't stand him. She calls him a boring old fart and a snob, but then Della is only 19 and was now making faces behind his back.

'So what's it all about Bob?' I asked.

'I want you to write a book for me. You've done a fair bit of writing for me now, admittedly only articles on boxing, martial arts, cage fighting and so on but I like your style. Now it's time for your first book.'

I tried not to show how excited I was. I'd waited a long time for this but I reasoned silently to myself Bob had access to many clever writers who have stacks of high sellers under their belts, why me? Why take a risk with me? When I asked his reply was; 'because you're young. That's the angle on this one. I want a totally new approach.'

'What's the subject, Bob?'

He leant back in his chair and lit a cigarette, drew on it and blew a large cloud of smoke rings. 'What does JFK mean to you?'

My brain went blank. Della butted in 'Furniture, the big furniture store that went bust.'

'That's MFI you stupid bitch!' There were times when being good (in fact very good) in bed wasn't everything. If you want intelligent conversation include Della out.

'I'm not taking that crap from you, Dan!' she yelled at the top of her voice. 'And that destructive, horrible parrot of yours has chewed up and shit on my stage costume. That's going to cost you. It's getting close to when you're going to have to choose between me and that bird. It wouldn't be so bad if it was house trained! For Christ sake! So crunch time for big beak ain't far off pal!'

'Don't ask me to choose between you and Mickey, Della. You can only come second.'

With that she went ballistic; a volley of abuse, and this time for good. She screamed and followed it with a string of foul language followed by heavy door slamming. Then she was gone.

Bob looked embarrassed. 'Don't worry about it Bob, she'll be back tomorrow. Now JFK, yes, the American President. The poor guy got murdered by a gunman. What does the F stand for?'

'John Fitzgerald Kennedy,' he said with a sigh.

There was a long pause. 'Yeah, to be honest Bob I don't think I can do it, sorry. I know nothing about American politics. I don't even bother to vote in my own country and anyway he was killed over 25 years before I was born! And there's a lot of books out there on who they think killed him.'

'There's more than a lot, Daniel. At the last count, on Amazon alone, there were nearly 8,000 on Kennedy, most of them about the assassination.'

'So the World needs another one?'

'Yes it does. One from a totally new angle and more to the point totally new info. And from the viewpoint of a young person of today. You can bring it in Daniel; I regard you as a literary Mickey Rourke. You're not carrying any preconceived ideas. The bottom line is that although some of the books, movies and documentaries are brilliant, most are rubbish, and not one has come up with a real cast iron answer as to who killed him and above all, why?'

'And you have that answer, Bob?'

'I have information as to who found out the real truth and what happened to that truth and who is suppressing it to this very day.'

'Mmm I'm interested man, sounds like the real deal to me. I'll tell you what, Bob, let's go for it.' He smiled for the first time since he'd arrived. Not that he smiles much and he laughs even less.

'OK let's take it steady. I'll feed you the information slowly. I got it when I was in New York earlier this week and it's still coming in. I'll give you the names of six people;

they are the main players in this tale of murder and wickedness on a massive scale. So you remember JFK. But you admit you don't know a lot about him. OK, Barack Obama?'

'Sure, he's the President over there. They were all saying he was going to put the World right in a matter of days. Well he's been in for around three years. I wonder how long the honeymoon's going to last?'

'OK now, what about Johnnie Ray?'

I thought hard and then said, 'No, never heard of him.'

'OK, Dorothy Kilgallen?'

'Likewise, Bob, the name means zero to me.'

'Lee Oswald and Jack Ruby?'

'No, sorry, doesn't ring any bells. Do you still want me to write this?' We both laughed. 'Here, give me your glass, what'll you have?' I asked.

'A double whisky no ice. Do you have Grouse?'

'Sure I do, I'll have another myself.'

I took his glass, then said, 'Hey, wait just a minute. I don't know Ruby but did that Oswald have a sort of middle name?'

'Yes he did. Lee Harvey Oswald.'

'Didn't they say he shot the President? I saw a photo long, long ago. He was handcuffed to a cop. They were leaving a building and a guy puts a revolver right up close to his chest and fires. He doubles up in pain, slumped down to the ground and he's gone, rather like I did in round three of my last fight. I can't take anymore beatings in the ring Bob. Let me do this book and as I know sweet fuck-all about the subject, I'll do it for half the fee of any of your other writers.'

'Don't crawl Daniel it doesn't suit you.'

He took an envelope from his inside pocket and tossed it over to me. 'Here's two grand in advance to cover expenses. After that you're on a pound a book in the UK and fifty pence for all overseas sales. My other writers wouldn't touch it as a gift; the subject's too dangerous and they're all getting on. You're young, can take care of yourself and even more to the point you're half nuts due to all those head punches you've been taking in the ring.'

'Thanks Bob, anybody else would have said completely nuts.'

'And for the record Daniel, the guy in that photo shooting Oswald is Jack Ruby.'

He stayed a couple more hours. We got the better of a bottle of whisky and had some laughs. As he put on his coat to leave he gave me my instructions.

'Right give me a word picture first of all on Johnnie Ray. Go and see Terry Cunningham, he's written several books for me. He did one years ago about recording artists of the 1950's. It's long out of print. He'll know all about

Johnnie Ray. Terry only lives about a mile or so from here in Bloomsbury.'

'So this Ray was in show business?'

'You bet he was; a singer, a superstar of his day. Get back to me when you've seen Terry. Here, here's his phone number,' he handed me a card.

'You're not telling me JFK was shot by a singer because he couldn't get his latest record in the charts?'

'I'm not telling you anything. It's for you to find out. Now go to it or leave it.'

'I'll go to it and give it my best shot, Bob.'

'Oh, before I go study this.' He handed me a DVD. 'It's a real life movie of JFK's last moments. You see him getting killed, it's awful. And this will come in very useful; a small pocket size voice activated recorder, record your info then type it up later.'

'Thanks Bob.'

'Don't thank me, the cost will come out of your first pay check.'

'One last question. Do you want me to go over to the States?'

'No that's part of the angle, an outsider's view. Americans are even now too close to it. I'll bring America to you. Have you been there?'

'Sure, one of my uncles, James, went straight from Ireland to New York. Lived in the Bronx all his life. I loved visiting him. He's buried up in St Saviour's cemetery. Another time I went right out to the West Coast by Greyhound bus. Still trying to get over it.'

Bob laughed again. I say there's nothing like getting in solid with the boss, especially when he's just handed you a two grand advance in wages that I put in my secret hiding place in case money mad Della saw it, or worse still got her hands on it.

The next day Della had got over her sulks and borrowed my car to go to a dance audition so I called Zian, a Chinese guy who drives, or maybe I should say pedals, a rickshaw. There are plenty of them on the Soho streets. He's based down in Gerrard Street and that's China Town. I made a note of his number when he put a trade card through my door about a month ago. He always seems to be available and was at my place in less than ten minutes. A London black cab would take three times that. 'Russell Square, Zian, my old pal.'

'You bet Mr Dan,' I sat back and enjoyed the hair raising ride, amazed at how Zian took us up on the pavements, scattering yelling pedestrians, down bus only lanes and the wrong way down at least two one way streets. When I pointed this out his answer was 'Well I'm only going one way!' Yeah right!

Chapter 2 – The Very First Rock 'n' Roller

Terry's flat was old fashioned and cosy, looking out on busy Russell Square. We had heard of each other but never met until now. He made me welcome, and his charming wife brought us in tea on a silver tray. With Jack Russell "Sandy" on his lap he settled back on the sofa.

'Do you mind if I record our chat?' I showed him the recorder Bob gave me.

'Sure go ahead, I use one myself.'

'Bob said you saw Johnnie Ray on stage.'

'Yes, several times. First time was in 1953 at the London Palladium then in the 60's when he toured with Judy Garland, and later still in Las Vegas. And I interviewed him for a music magazine, but his great days were well and truly over by then.'

'You know, Terry, they say those giant Sequoia trees in California are the oldest living things on earth.'

He looked confused 'Yes, so I've heard.'

'Well I think they're wrong. You must be even older.' He started to laugh, sipped his tea and sighed.

'Yes, I guess 1953 must seem a long while ago to someone your age. But I recall it far better than what happened last week.'

'So tell me, who the hell was Johnnie Ray?'

'Well, to understand the colossal impact Ray had on music and the world of entertainment, I must try and describe those times to you,' he paused and then said 'It won't be easy. Were you born here?' he asked.

'Yes my family and parents are all Irish but I was born and raised a Londoner.'

'Well,' he continued 'the London you know, and that I knew back in the fifties, are totally different in almost every way, utterly different. Back then it was drab, dull and poor. Entertainment wise we had the cinema of course, there was no TV.

Our parents listened to the popular big bands on radio: Harry James, Stan Kenton, and many others. They put out some great music but they'd been around since the 1930's. Then in 1951 it changed overnight, and forever. The age of the lone singer came in. The age of the solo recording star had arrived.

The first over was Frankie Laine. He stayed a big star until he died in 2007 and was followed by another multimillion seller, Guy Mitchell. They all came over to top the bill at the Palladium: Nat King Cole, Tennessee Ernie and the girl singers too, all multi million sellers. There was Jo Stafford, Teresa Brewer, Kay Starr, Doris Day. They played to sell-out tours, queues round the block to get tickets to see them, standing room only.

Then came the biggest star of all, Johnnie Ray. You had to be there to believe it. At that time he was probably by far the biggest name on the planet. An absolute showbiz sensation, he looked good; tall thin blonde, the guy exploded onto the stage, down on his knees, playing the piano, going into the audience with a hand mic. He wore one of those old style hearing aids, you know, the lead going from his ear down to a mike clipped to his coat pocket.'

'That's what I'd call a great gimmick!'

'No he really was very deaf. Take a listen to this, I dug it out when you said you were calling in.' He got up and put a CD on the stereo. It was a live show. You could hear the hysteria and frenzy coming across. Beatle mania in the 1960's had nothing on this. We listened to two numbers; "Somebody Stole my Girl" and "Whisky and Gin".

'Man that's Rock n Roll if ever I heard it', I said.

'You're dead right, he was the first Rock n Roller. Every night after his show the crowds, thousands of them, would block Argyll Street where the Palladium is and the traffic would be blocked up in Regent Street right up to Oxford Circus. The police lost control of the crowds. He was without doubt a totally original artist with a unique style he made his own. No other singer ever tried to copy him. There are many would-be Tony Bennett's or Frank Sinatra's but no-one tried to copy Johnnie. His first hit "Cry", recorded in '51, was one of the most intensely powerful records ever made. I'd say it had more impact on music at that time, than ever Elvis did with "Heartbreak Hotel" five years later. He had the same massive impact on music that James Dean had on the movies in '54.'

'Talking of Dean, I read your book on him. Loved it, I'm a fan.'

'Thank you Dan, when Elvis was doing his fabulous Las Vegas show around, I think, 1971, Ray was in the audience, I was there too that night. Elvis stopped the show saying "Ladies and gentlemen there's a singer in the audience tonight. One of the greatest artists of our time. In my last year at school he had numbers 1, 2 and 3 in the hit parade. He had a great effect on me, making me believe in myself and making me what I am today. Please give a warm welcome to Mr Johnnie Ray." The audience gave Ray a standing ovation.'

'That was praise indeed from Elvis.'

'It sure was, what really hit his career bad was when the press found out he was gay. Today no one would give a damn but back then it was illegal and it killed his movie career, great shame, he was a natural on screen. He had a very strong fan base over here in the UK. He came over several times for Royal Command performances but he hit a downward spiral, started to drink real heavy. The whole thing went to pieces, his career I mean. A lady he had a long relationship with was found murdered in New York and he never got over it, least that's the way I heard it.'

'But didn't you say he was gay?'

'Well I don't know, I guess he swung both ways, bisexual.'

'And you did an interview with him?'

'Yeah I called at the theatre. They said he has just gone to lunch and I found him with a friend in a run down café across the street having a tea and sandwich and no one even recognised him.

He was pleasant to talk to no big star crap; his pal had to explain my questions because he was so severely deaf. He said those shit doctors told him they could cure his hearing loss and operated and made it worse. Then there was op number two to correct their mistake and this time they took away most of the hearing that was left, and left him with nerve-racking Tinnitus. Like the old saying Terry, "The operation was a success but the patient died."

When he was making big money he gave a lot to hearing charities, he looked a care worn man like he was carrying a burden. We reminisced about the 1950's. He told me in the late 1960's he went bankrupt. All the years of touring, TV, million selling records and he was skint; lousy managers, agents and of course the taxes had wiped him out.

Also Frank Sinatra sabotaged his career because he had a fling with movie star Ava Gardner. Career wise big mistake.'

'Sort of mistake I'd like to make Terry!'

'Yes we should be so lucky, but she was Sinatra's girl; old blue eyes never forgot it, and he owned Reprise Records, Ray's record label, so made sure Johnnie's new work never got released.

Then he mentioned that lady he loved very much and how she'd died in New York. But he would never buy that; he said he knew she was murdered. This will interest you Dan, he told me she found out why Kennedy was killed. When I asked him to tell me more, he said *believe me you don't want to know. If the American government knew what she told me I'd be killed like she was*. I put it down at the time to a bit of fantasy, you know what showbiz people are like. When I said goodbye he shook my hand warmly saying not to mention what he'd told me about Dorothy, at least not until I've been dead a hundred years.'

'Who was she?'

'She was a powerful newspaper and television woman who found out something about the Kennedy assassination. She must have found out too much and got too close to the truth.'

'What was her full name?'

'Dorothy Kilgallen. Not known over here but real big time Stateside.'

'Hey, that's one of the names Bob wants me to check out.'

'Well Dan, I won't say too much about her for the simple reason I don't know very much. Bob can connect you with people who can tell you a lot more than I can. By the way, are you any connection with a boxer from way back called Eric McQuade, a south London welter weight?'

'Yeah he's a distant relative and his younger brother Pat was also a fighter.'

'They were good Dan; I saw them fight many times. Now how about a bite to eat?'

'No thanks, I've got to go. You've been a great help with all the Johnnie Ray info. Apart from your other books, do you still write about music?'

'No, I'm too old and I don't, and never will, understand Rap.'

We laughed. As I got up to leave he looked serious and said 'You know a few years back, I wrote a book about the '14-18 war and I revealed some facts about how our politicians had shares in armament factories and ended up ten times richer after the war than when it started. It was banned by every library in the country, even prison libraries wouldn't touch it, nor would bookshops. Only Amazon on-line were brave enough to carry it.'

I must have looked puzzled because he smiled and continued. 'My point being if they can crush new info about 1914, what chance will your book about 1963 stand? That's only like the day before yesterday to those swines. They'll come out of the woodwork to kill your book the day it's printed, and more to the point they will do all they can to stop it ever seeing the light of day!

So watch yourself son and trust no one. I wish you luck with this Kennedy book and really look forward to reading it.'

We shook hands before he gave me an affectionate hug. As I went down in the lift I keyed in Zian's number to come and get me and stood waiting in the entrance doorway keeping out of the rain, thinking about this singer who once stopped London's traffic, and was the biggest name on the planet.

Now if I was to ask one of these people hurrying by in the rain to catch their trains what they know about Johnnie Ray they wouldn't even know the name. For some strange reason it made me feel sad.

Zian's rickshaw skidded to a stop with the back wheels locked. I climbed in and sat well back in the seat, then told Zian about the Johnnie Ray story making me feel sort of depressed.

'Ahh Mr Dan, *ask not for whom the bell tolls*' Zian said.

'Yeah, you know Zian, on late night TV they show old movies. A famous one is *Charley Chan Chinese Detective*. He goes around solving crimes and like you he's always coming out with great quotes, but he starts by saying "Confucius he say", then the quote, why don't you do that?'

'Because, Mr Dan that one was by English poet John Donne. Not Confucius. Where to Mr Dan?'

'After that put down let's go to the gym and have a work out.'

Zian holds a 7th degree in Aikido and is a kick boxing instructor. The gym was full of fat minders, security guards, cops and other assorted arseholes all trying to look the business and fooling no one. I did four hard K.B rounds with Zian and some judo with his attractive girlfriend Jia-Li who is lightning fast and, like most women, could, in the right or maybe wrong situation be very dangerous.

After a shower and Chinese tea Zian peddled me and Jia-Li home. That's right, he peddled hard and fast pulling me at just over 10 stone and Jia-Li who's a petite maybe 8 stone, when he weighs in at around just over 9 stone. He's one mean hard strong fighter who can punch way above his weight with ease.

Chapter 3 – Mickey Vs. Della

Whenever I enter my flat Mickey greets me with 'Hello Dan', but if someone else is there he stays silent and just looks in the direction of the other person. Why he does this is a mystery known only to Macaws.

So the first thing I noticed was Mickey's silence, and the way he was perched on top of the cage, feathers bunched up with his head down a sure sign he was in a deep sulk. I knew why when Della suddenly appeared from the kitchen in a haze of French perfume and naked except for high heels. She made a habit of walking around the flat that way, much to my enjoyment I have to say.

'I thought you were never going to return?' I asked.

'That was yesterday, but I can shove off if you want.'

'No stay,' I replied. I couldn't take my eyes off her massive breasts, tiny waist and long, long legs. Within a matter of minutes, no seconds, we were locked in each others arms on my king size bed. Screwing like there was no tomorrow. She brought me to a climax in no time and we lay together gazing at the dark starless night sky outside my window.

'You were in such a hurry you forgot to draw the blinds,' she laughed.

'Well if anyone was watching I think we put on a great show. Next time I'll sell tickets first.' We could hear the beat of wings and loud squawks as Mickey flew from room to room trying to find me. He finally settled on top of the half open bedroom door looking down on us with what I thought was an evil eye.

'That bird hates me,' said Della.

'Macaws,' I told her, 'are one person birds and very possessive of their owners. Also they are the only animal that has learnt to speak our language. And don't ever put your hand in or on his cage, he only lets me do that because he regards that as his territory.'

'Yeah, yeah. That's really, really interesting,' said Della stifling a mock yawn. 'His territory is the Amazon jungle why don't you send the big shit back there? I'll even pay his fare.'

'Yeah, with my money,' I responded.

'Anyway I forgot to tell you, Bob phoned. He wants you to contact some woman in the States. I've written it all down for you on the jotter on your desk, it's to do with the book you're doing for him. How you doing with it?'

'I've not written a word yet but I'm making stacks of notes and seeing people who can tell me about those involved with the story.'

'Why can't those involved tell you?'

'Because most of them are dead', I answered vaguely. I was already wondering if I could make love to her once more. She looked gorgeous in the soft light filling the room from the neon signs in Oxford Street. The more meaningful reply to her question would have been that they were all murdered or died very mysteriously. She worked me up slowly in a way that any man would die for, then got astride me, saying she'll do the work this time.

After a few minutes of sheer ecstasy she let out a piecing scream, I felt pleased that she found me such a good lover. But she followed the scream with; 'That fucking no good shit of a bird! This time it's neck gets wrung!'

Mickey had flown down and bitten Della's arse hard. Our passion came to an abrupt end. Della chased after Mickey grabbing the broom on the way. And Mickey, giving out ear splitting squawks and fearing being beaten to death by an enraged pole dancer, had landed on the highest point in the flat, the kitchen curtain rail.

I chased after her snatching the broom handle just in time. We retired to the bathroom where I bathed her arse cheek with cold water and placed a large sticking plaster over the bite.

'I won't be able to work for weeks! Who ever saw a pole dancer with a big band aid on her arse,' she sobbed.

'Tell them it was your lover who bit you. Could give your act a whole new slant,' I suggested. 'Here, this will tide you over.' I gave her £500 out of the two grand Bob had given me.

'I mean it this time Dan, that bird goes or I don't return! It's not a domestic animal, like a dog or cat, it belongs in the jungle. That big beak of his could take your hand off.'

I called Zian on my mobile to collect her and take her home. At the door she turned, gave me a quick kiss on the cheek and put my spare door key I'd given her in my hand; maybe her way of saying its over.

Some time later I read the note from Bob, "Contact Maria Moretti", there followed an email address and phone numbers. "She can give us priceless info on Dorothy Kilgallen. She's expecting your call. Tread carefully, she has a short fuse. Make sure you're alone when you speak to her, nobody but you must hear what she is going to tell you."

Mickey was now perched on the back of my chair. I leant back and stroked his head saying 'You've been a wicked old bird again but I forgive you.' I then gave him a couple of his favourite cashew nuts. Bob's note gave a time of 2.40am to call Maria. I guess to allow for the time difference. We were to talk via the web cam. As it was still an hour away I took a shower and lay on my bed making notes of what questions to ask this mysterious lady.

Chapter 4 – Dorothy Kilgallen

On the webcam Maria looked an attractive Afro American, maybe late middle aged. Her accent had a slight southern drawl.

'So you're a fighter Dan?'

'I used to be. My last fight was a couple of months ago and I got the shit knocked out of me. Since then I've turned to cage fighting, well it pays the rent. I really want to break into writing. This JFK book is my big chance.'

'Quit boxing now or you'll end up a stumble bum, that's our term for a broken down punch-drunk fighter. You have a good publisher in Bob at *Stagedoor*, he looks out for those on his team. I worked with him on a book about James Dean and came over to London to do 'London Street Girls' all about crime in your city.'

'Sounds like a dangerous project.'

'It was nothing like this JFK you're taking on. I was up against local gangsters, you're taking on the sinister international establishments. You're getting into a cage now Dan to fight the most powerful forces on earth.'

'I'm glad you didn't say it's no contest. Anyway I don't scare that easy Maria, I'll take my chances.'

She gave what I thought was a sad smile then said 'OK that's the small talk over. By now you know all about

Johnnie Ray, now it's Dorothy Kilgallen time. She was a lovely elegant lady, her father was a famous newspaper reporter and she followed him right to the top. I was only a poor coloured kid starting out in journalism so you can imagine some of the shit I had to deal with back then, but she treated me with respect. She started out in Hollywood writing about the movies and the stars, then came back East to work in her home town, New York. Her husband was Richard Kollmar, big time show bizz agent and Broadway impresario. They lived in a magnificent five storey town house at 45 East 68th Street, off Fifth Avenue, where they gave lavish parties. They had their own very popular radio show called "Breakfast with Dorothy and Dick". Radio was very big in those pre TV days. When TV did come in, she starred in a show that ran for many years called "What's my Line" '.

'So Maria, although not known over here, she was big Stateside?'

'Dan we are talking real big and powerful with it. If Dorothy was calling the President of the day would leave an important meeting to take her call. But her first love was being a newspaper woman. Her twice weekly column appeared in every major newspaper coast to coast.'

'I get the feeling you liked her.'

'You better believe it. Things were very racist in those days and years later I heard that her editor had warned her it could harm her image to be seen taking a poor coloured girl under her wing. She told him if she liked someone who has talent and needed a helping hand she didn't give a damn who or what they were. I went to her house a couple of times; she would edit articles I wrote for magazines. All sorts of famous people would be there and I was too shy to open my mouth. I guess she knew that and quietly gave me confidence. Sadly I never followed through with the faith she had in me.'

'Why do you say that Maria?'

'Well, to be honest I never had her sheer talent, very few did. Also things went wrong in my private life; you know how it is Dan.' (We both laughed. It was the laughter of mutual understanding.)

'So how would you sum her up?'

'In a word, "integrity". That girl had it by the truckload; a good mother to her three kids that she adored; ladylike always dressed kinda nice; polite, didn't swear. And where a newspaper story was concerned she would follow through to the bitter end and wouldn't be warned off, or scared off by no one. She would want the truth and nothing but. She would say to me "My readers deserve nothing less. The bus driver here in NY, the car worker in Detroit, the cowboy in Arizona and their wives and families have a right to know exactly what's going on".'

'Do you think that had something to do with her strange death?'

'I don't mince words Dan. I damn well know it did. Dorothy was murdered, no two ways about it. I've thought about this more over the years than I care to admit, even to myself, and spoken to many people who were close to her and I can tell you why she was murdered.'

'OK Maria let me in on it.'

'I'm not talking about who pulled the trigger and all that shit about the Mafia, the CIA (Central Intelligence Agency) the FBI (Federal Bureau of Investigation) or Castro, Freemasons, the Russians, and a whole crowd more. Now listen close Dan and this applies to JFK as well as Dorothy. Everyone since 1963 from Governments to the man in the street has been asking who killed them, when they should have been asking WHY were they killed?

To attempt a crime of that magnitude you must have a reason of equal or greater magnitude. I know in my heart that Doll was killed because of what she knew, and JFK also knew the same thing and just maybe refused to go along with it.'

'What do you think it was? Or at least give me an educated guess.'

'I'd give the World to know the answer Dan but sadly I don't. But it must have been truly horrendous. Jack Ruby was not high up enough to know, he was just another gunman but he must have told Doll something that sent her investigative mind into overdrive. And you asked what was the reason? Well whatever it was is still with us, the powers that be are still intimidating and killing to keep it under wraps.'

'But those responsible back in '63 would no longer be around Maria.'

'No so it must be something that is handed on from one generation to the next. Let me tell you about what you're getting into. I let it be known that I wanted to do a book about Dorothy and her mysterious death. I got repeated phone calls telling me to forget it. I told the callers to get lost. Then my US publisher was found hanged. They tried to say he was trying some weird sexual trick that went wrong. Bullshit, he was a straight up beat guy. No way would he die that way or any other way.

I come from New Orleans. I know it like the back of my hand so I'm driving down town when a car pulls level with me and shots ring out; the back and side windows are blown out. I put my foot down but a second car pulls in behind and tries to ram me onto the sidewalk, but my little Honda can outmanoeuvre them. I cut down a dozen side streets and lose them.

So I leave town in a hurry. An ex-boyfriend truck driver takes me way out to Duluth, Wisconsin and I hide out for a month in a small nearby town called Minong working on my book. They even trace me there, tell me to stop the book and hand over what I'd done so far or my granddaughter at college gets killed. So no contest, I give up.'

'That's one trick they can't pull on me. I have no close family. All I know is that the lady died in very mysterious circumstances, can you tell me more Maria?'

'Sure, when Jack Ruby, the guy who shot Lee Harvey Oswald, was arrested, he was taken to the cells at the Dallas Police Department. The police plus the entire world wanted to know why he did it. He refused to talk to anyone or give any explanation. After a few days he said "OK I'll talk to one person, the only person out there that I'd trust. Get me Dorothy Kilgallen."

She flew down from New York and they had several meetings alone, just the two of them. She never made public what Ruby had told her. She kept all her notes in a large folder that she never let out of her sight. But she did say publicly "The information that has come my way via Jack Ruby is dynamite and I shall use it to blow this case of our President's murder sky high and wide open."

Having studied this for years I feel sure she told the four people she could trust most in her life, with her life, because that's what she was doing and they never betrayed that trust. In fact three of them died sooner than reveal what she told them.

The only one who died of natural causes was Johnnie Ray because the forces of evil made the big mistake of underestimating him. With his country boy charm he fooled them into thinking he was just another entertainer friend of hers. If they realised how close he and Doll were he would have died a violent death like so many others.

'I know about Johnnie and I'd like to know more about her friends that she trusted, but first tell me about how Doll died?'

'The whole thing was weird, totally unreal. She was only 52, came home late from doing her TV show, her husband and her young son were in the house, she said she was going to work on her book and the interviews with Jack Ruby.

Well she had a large bedroom with a smaller bedroom adjoining it on the top floor; she always slept in the small room. She was found fully dressed sitting up in bed in the main bedroom, she even had her false eyelashes still on. That would be an absolute no-no for Doll, the book came out after her death titled "Murder One" about the famous murder trials she had attended over the years as a crime reporter, but of course the biggest story of all, Jack Ruby's, was missing.'

'So you're saying Maria, her murderers got it wrong, and the whole scene stinks.'

'You bet. The verdict as to the cause of death by the ME's office and Medical Examiner Dominick DiMaio was "Undetermined", in other words they didn't know how she came to be dead! DiMaio signed the death certificate, but years later in 1995 he made a statement saying he did not sign it, someone forged his signature, he never set foot in Dorothy's house.

They did find small amounts of Seconal in her body but not enough to kill her. The FBI and CIA had been hounding her since she interviewed Jack Ruby, kept taking her in for some heavy questioning, her house was under 24 hour surveillance and her phones were tapped. There were no mobiles back then so she made calls from clubs, restaurants and even a call box along the street. She told a fellow reporter that her mail was being opened and read before being delivered. Dick, her husband, was asleep two floors below when the killers got in quietly and got to the top floor. They had come to kill her before she blew the works, but also to get that folder. Knowing Doll she didn't have it or refused to say who did have it so they killed her. These people have sophisticated ways of killing without leaving any trace. Remember forensic science was not as advanced as it is today. They spent time searching her rooms from top to bottom. But left empty handed.'

'What did this folder look like Maria?'

'Well I saw it once when I called to see her. She was working on the Jack Ruby section of her book. I never read any of it but you know when you buy a pack of legal size copy paper, well kinda like the size of that, and kept in a black soft leather brief case. Now Dan ask yourself why JFK was shot? You must have a damn good reason to order the assassination of the President of the USA. Presidents come and go, they're voted in and out, so to kill him in broad daylight in front of millions. Man it must be because you have no alternative. There must have been something he refused to do or refused point blank to go along with.

Don't look, Dan, for who pulled the trigger. Look for the reason the trigger was pulled.'

'Tell me, Maria, who do you think she gave the folder containing the Ruby interview and other stuff to?'

'Well first you have to realise there were no computers, no home photocopying machines. All Doll would have had, even a top flight journalist like her, would be a typewriter. In fact, I recall a big new Electric Underwood on her desk so most or all those notes would be written in longhand. She couldn't just dash off a few copies and no way could she take them to her newspaper office to copy. She had two live in staff; a married couple and a personal maid Marie Eichler who came in two or three days a week, who I got to know quite well. Now she told me that Doll asked her to take a package to the post office addressed to

Johnnie Ray, who was out in California at the time, two or three days before Doll was murdered. Marie said Doll was real desperate about that parcel, sent me by cab and told me to send it express air mail special delivery.

Marie also told me it was she who found the body, not Doll's hairdresser as stated in the police report. She came in early to get Doll ready for a photo shoot she was doing later that day. I'd bet my life Dan that was the folder she posted, she knew her killers were closing in, and out of all the four people closest and most trusted in her life he would be the last one they would suspect; a show biz person with no interest in politics.

The ones they did suspect were all systematically killed. Even poor Marie was grilled by the CIA and the FBI but she stuck to her story that she knew nothing. And said not a word about the parcel sent to Johnnie. I recall she told me she was a fan, had all his records and liked him very much as a person. "Why I'd never cause that sweet guy any trouble, and I could sense it was real big trouble of some sort and Miss Kilgallen was the best lady I ever worked for so I reckoned I owed her." But for all that Dan, Marie disappeared soon after, never to be seen alive again. A fellow crime reporter told me she was pulled out of the East river weeks later, but listed as Marie *Eicher*, that's why I couldn't trace her. That misspelt name was deliberate you can bet.

Dan I gotta go, I hand it all over to you. All us 1963 people are too old to bring this in. It needs someone young like you so take it and run with it, but I fear for you man. They will soon be looking for you so keep your head down and good luck.'

'Thanks Maria for all this info. I've enough notes now to start work proper. But one last question. Who were the other three people she trusted so much?'

'OK, her husband Richard Kollmar, Mary Meyer and Florence Smith.'

'Did you know them?'

'Her husband slightly, but not the two women.'

'Thanks Maria, I hope we speak again sometime soon.'

I shut down the computer and, putting my feet against the desk, pushed my office chair back on its wheels. I'd been looking at the monitor for well over two hours. My eyes felt tired. Not bothering to undress I got a few hours restless sleep.

Chapter 5 – Who The Hell Are You Zian?

The light from the balcony window woke me. Last night, while Maria was talking I'd been letting my recorder run and making notes like crazy on a stack of photocopying paper. So now I wanted to highlight certain sections of what she had told me but my yellow marker pen was not in its usual place in the right hand draw.

'What have you done with it Mickey?' He was in his favourite place on my shoulder. I asked him this because he likes nothing better than to pick up objects, like pens, take them back to his cage and chew them to pieces. Before I could question him further my phone rang, it was Zian.

'You not come to gym? You not win next fight if you don't train Mr Dan.'

'Sorry Zian I had work to do on the book.'

'Yes, how you get on with book?'

'Yeah, making progress.'

'It enormous subject, biggest unsolved murder of century Mr Dan.'

'You know about JFK Zian?'

'Sure of course. I know lot about him. He great President. Like all of us he had feet of clay, he liked the ladies maybe too much but great man for America. He wanted the best for his country, when I at college in Shanghai we study lot about American history.'

'Well when you call round next you can help answer some questions I forgot to ask an American lady I've just been talking to on the web-cam.'

'Sure will Mr Dan. Must go now, have to take fare to American embassy in Grosvenor square.'

'Where from?'

'I collect her from Hotel in the Strand.'

'Man that's some haul. You are one super fit people peddler. I hope she's real light weight.'

'Hard work good for soul, work is ultimate salvation Mr Dan.'

'Did Confucius say that?'

'No it's from your Bible!'

'Well if you don't drop dead from hard work I'll see you soon my mad Chinese pal.'

I went back to my pen search and found it in the left hand draw of my desk, somewhere I never put it. Maybe Della had been looking in my desk for something, but then again I don't think so.

I suddenly felt in need of some fresh air and decided to take up Zian's invite to the gym. I ran down the narrow four flights of stairs. As I approached the street door I saw a hand written notice pinned to it. "Please Make Sure This Door Is Shut Tight When You Leave. Thank You". Stuck at the back of the hall light switch there was a letter waiting for me.

It was from my fight manager, a short note saying I must start winning more cage fights and a cheque for £1100. £500 for a fight I won and £300 each for two I lost. As those fights were spread over six weeks that's around £180 a week, not exactly big time. As I put the cheque in my wallet I heard Barney's voice calling me.

Barney is a lovely old Jewish tailor that I've known for years, who works on the ground floor and always has a stubby cigar stuck in his mouth.

'Danny boy!'

'Hi Barney.'

'Danny please, please tell your lady friends to shut this door tight. You have to pull it hard.'

'Yeah, when I tell them I'll make sure they know I mean the door.'

'Very funny Dan, but if that door is only half closed any weirdo out there can get into the building.'

'OK, but Della knows about the door.'

'Yes, Della, she is OK lady but Dan you have other ladies in you busy life who don't shut the door OK. So tell them please.'

'Not these days Barney you won't believe it but I'm writing a book and it's taking all my time; no time for fun and games.'

'Your love life none of my business young man and a couple of months ago I made you a lovely suit so why you kid me.'

'I love the suit Barney. You're an artist but Della is the only one right now and that's only when the mood takes me. Honest.'

'So who is the pretty blonde lady? She sure ain't visiting me. I don't do ladies work.'

'Tell me about her Barney.'

'Well she maybe late twenties, slim, blonde hair in swept up style. She wear red jacket tight black skirt and high heels, black shoulder bag.'

'Apart from that you really didn't notice her right? She's nothing to do with me Barney, I wish she were. If I'm lucky enough to see her I'll tell her about the door. Here's £200 deposit. Make me a sports jacket in dark blue lightweight material, you've got my measurements.'

'Danny for you I have something extra special, a jacket length of Vicuna.' 'What's that Barney?'

'Only the finest material in the World and not being made anymore, and terrible expensive but as it fell off the back of a lorry, for you a very special price.'

'Sometimes Barney your special prices make me think the cloth fell off the back of a Rolls Royce.'

'You kid me Danny. Look you walk over to Mayfair and you pay ten times the price I charge for same thing.'

'OK that's for me. Can I pay in instalments? Spread over 25 years?'

'Sure, because I not only like you, I trust you.' He laughed as he turned to go back to his workroom and called out; 'There ain't nothing in the World like being young so enjoy it Danny boy.'

I grabbed a cab to Holborn and as I entered the gym Zian greeted me.

'Hello Mr Dan I am pleased you change mind. Let's have work out.'

We did some kick boxing and judo but after 45 minutes I began to tire and sensed Zian was going easy on me.

'Your heart not in fighting anymore Mr Dan?'

'Sorry Zian, guess I'm getting old,' he laughed.

'Your mind is on other things, my friend, a quick shower then we jog back to Jia-Li's place and you have meal with us at her Father's restaurant.'

As we made our way through the dull wet backstreets to Lyle Street I chatted about the book and for some reason I mentioned about the sexy blonde that Barney said wasn't shutting our street door.

At this Zian fell silent and just said 'When you go home tonight I come with you.' I ached like hell after the workout so it was good to relax at Jia-Li's place. Zian's a slim guy, around thirty years old, 5'9" tall who speaks quietly and moves quickly. Watching him work out is like watching an old movie of that dancing star Fred Astaire, you knew instinctively you were seeing someone at the top of their game.

Jia-Li and the other ladies moved off to another room to watch TV. Zian handed me a tall glass of Chinese tea. 'So what were questions you forgot to ask American lady?'

'Oh, obscure stuff you wouldn't know about.'

'Try me Mr Dan.'

'Before I do why the hell do you call me Mister Dan? Makes you sound like a servant and it makes me mad because no way can I afford a servant.'

Zian smiled. 'I come from another World so hard for you to understand but let's say I respect and like you. I regard you as a warrior fighting your way through life; it is not in any way subservient.'

'OK, if you say so. Yeah the questions, these people were the closest to Dorothy Kilgallen in her life and she trusted them. Tell me what happened to Florence Smith, Mary Meyer, and Richard Kollmar. But first I should ask if you know who Dorothy Kilgallen was and you won't, so lets talk about something else, I've had enough of JFK for one day OK.'

Zian took a sip of his tea and slowly put the glass back on the black marble table embossed with gold dragons; this went well with the black silk kimono he had put on as soon as we arrived.

'Kilgallen', he said slowly, 'was a fearless crusading journalist who, when taken in for questioning by the FBI and CIA, said she would never reveal source from where she was getting inside information on the JFK murder. So they threatened her with prison and generally made her life hell but she stood ground; a brave American and it cost her her life.'

Taken back by this quick and precise reply I paused for a minute then asked. 'And the others I mentioned, do you know what became of them?' And to my amazement he replied.

'I do indeed my friend and I tell you. Richard Kollmar, her husband, was hounded by Government agencies and destroyed both professionally and socially. He was murdered in his house after Dorothy, in the same room and in much the same way. The verdict was suicide. Florence Smith had been friends with Dorothy for many years. In her young life she was Florence Pritchett, very pretty fashion model and actress, she had an affair with JFK when in their twenties. She married Earl Smith ambassador to Cuba, and she lived only few streets away from Dorothy. And she dies very mysteriously just two days after Dorothy die. She only 45. Verdict; cause of death unknown. Mary Meyer also very beautiful lady, she knew JFK when at

49

college, they had long love affair when both young. But for rest of life she stay close to JFK and visit him many time at White House when his wife Jackie away. Her maiden name was Mary Pinchot. She work as artist and mix with artistic people, she big friend of Dorothy and, like Florence, give her inside information on what goes on in White House. She married to Cord Meyer, he World War Two hero so he get job with CIA. A few months after JFK murder Mary go for walk with dog along riverbank near her home in Georgetown Washington D.C, she found dead; shot once in head and once in heart, she only 44. No sign of robbery or sexual assault. Verdict; killed by persons unknown. Her husband Cord on his death bed in 2001 said, "My wife was murdered by same evil people that killed the President".

We both sat quietly for a few minutes drinking our tea, it was very peaceful in this oriental style room, we could have been a million miles from noisy, brash Soho that was outside the front door. I broke the silence by asking:

'Just who the hell are you Zian? And if you say you're a rickshaw driver I'll kick box your fucking head in.'

'Please Mr Dan do not swear in this house. By swearing here you show me and others who dwell here no respect.'

'Yeah I'm out of order sorry I'll clear off. I gotta visit someone.'

'No need to go Mr Dan. Stay, have some food. Jia-Li making meal for us.'

'No I'll see ya.' With that I was back on Lyle Street. That big production by Zian about me swearing didn't fool me. OK, he's a polite guy and doesn't like bad language, but what he didn't like big time was me asking who he really is. The chances of a Chinese immigrant working as a rickshaw driver in London being an expert on murders surrounding the JFK mystery back in 1963 are around a billion to one. I don't buy it.

So all those people got taken out except Johnnie Ray. My bet is Dorothy sent the folder to him, like Maria said. So the World's first Rock n Roller was gay or bi and not political. Now what would he do with a folder that's a death sentence if they knew he had it? I know just the guy to give me an intelligent, educated guess.

Sebastian Horsley, he's like a modern day Quentin Crisp, or an olden days Oscar Wilde, known as the Dandy of Soho, wears flamboyant clothes, works as an artist and a very good one. His passion is painting sharks of all things. I keep hoping he'll sell me one if I can afford it. He even went out to Oz and swam in the pacific with those man eaters just to see them close up.

Another time he was painting something to do with crucifixion so, to experience the subject first hand, went to the Philippines and got himself crucified without painkillers, fell off the cross, the nails ripping his hands open, he nearly died. He keeps the nails on display in his flat as a souvenir.

Della and me have been to some of his wild parties; trouble is I'm not into drugs but Seb is a real heavy heroin addict. His flat is just a short walk away in Meard Street. I phoned first on the mobile and he sounded in good form; well you could never be sure with Seb, so I called round. He seemed pleased to see me but not quite with it.

'Let me get my head together Dan.' I watched as he poured two double whiskies and noticed his blue painted fingernails, his movie star good looks and flamboyant clothes. A few months ago a dealer had been threatening him for more drug money; Seb asked if I would help so I waited at his place and when the dealer came calling I punched half his face in, you'd think that would have got me a free painting as well as a fee, but no matter, Seb's entertainment value is priceless.

'Seb my old mate, I need the expert opinion of someone who knows the gay and bi scene.' I then related the whole story.

'Yes I know about Johnnie Ray. Long before my time of course but a superb entertainer. You know there is a big mystery about why, overnight, gay people came to be accepted. We went from being illegal and treated like shit to being popular, even fashionable. Take the media, one time you never saw us, now we're all over the place, the TV screens are full of gays. Many people said at the time around the late 70's that the gay community in San Francisco had something big on the US government. Only a rumour of course but maybe Johnnie gave the folder to an outfit that blackmailed the White House into changing things for gays and quick. It's a long shot but who knows, leave it with me Dan, I have contacts in high places. I'll ask around very discreetly and let you know as soon as I hear something.

So you're doing a book? I don't envy you. I found it very hard work when I wrote my life story back in 2007. A strange subject you've chosen I must say.'

'Why Seb?'

'Well is there anyone around who remembers Kennedy or cares who killed him? You see Darling we live in an age when no one cares about anything that happened further back than last week.'

'My angle, Seb, is not who killed him but why he was killed.'

'You could be getting in deep with that', he then started to laugh and said; 'Why not write about kinky sex and heavy drugs? My crowd would buy at least a million copies. Anyway wait till I tell you this. There's going to be a play about me right here in the West End.'

'That's fantastic Seb, I'm pleased for you.'

'Yes same title as my book; *Dandy in the Underworld*. It will all go to my head, I shall become quite impossible.' *As if you weren't already* I thought to myself. 'You know Dan, Soho's loosing its charm; 'PC' and 'elf- n- safety are killing the old place. It's about as wild and wicked now as suburbia. Do you know every square inch of Soho is now covered by CCTV? You're on camera, even if you're down a dark alley hiding behind a dustbin. The gangsters, musicians, actors, writers, artists, prostitutes are all moving out. Taking their place are boring pretentious corporate shits.'

My mobile rang, cutting off Seb in full rant, it was Della. 'I'm bringing back the car. Where are you? I'll pick you up.'

'I'm at Seb's place.'

Seb butted in, 'It's raining, could Della drop me off at the Groucho?'

'What happened to your favourite club the Colony?'

'It shut down', he said in a forlorn voice.

As the 'hat' is only a two seater Della sat on Sebs lap. He was wearing his top hat with a pink coloured suit, this drew some strange looks from equally strange people as we drove down Old Compton Street, better known as the gay highway, because of its clubs and bars.

I turned into Dean Street and as Della struggled to get out Seb squeezed her arse, 'Sorry dear boy, couldn't resist', Della gave him a playful slap.

54

'I'll find out all I can for you about Johnnie Ray and the missing folder. I know a VIP at the Yankee embassy, I mean a very important VIP.'

'Thanks pal, we struggling writers must stick together. You take care now Seb. I mean go easy on the crack and how about two tickets for your play?'

'Will do and send me tickets for your next cage fight. I just love seeing you knock the shit out of those dreadful people.'

'Trouble is Seb, those people are starting to knock it out of me.'

He laughed. 'Then it's time to stop dear boy', raised his top hat and with a swirl of his tailed pink coat was gone.

Dorothy and Johnnie, happy and in love, dining
out at the Waldorf-Astoria, New York, 1961.

Dorothy in her Hollywood days with her Angora cat *Cotton.*

Johnnie in London, 1953.

Dorothy at work in her office.

Johnnie Ray, World superstar, on stage at the London Palladium.

Dorothy with her husband Richard Kollmar. Both died
mysteriously in the same house in much the same way.

Dorothy and Richard.

Sebastian Horsley; artist, writer, raconteur.
The *Dandy of Soho*.

Look Homeward Angel – Johnnie Ray portrait by Mike Shaw.

Mary Meyer, artist and Bohemian, long time friend and lover of JFK.
Murdered 10 months after him. Also a close friend of
Dorothy Kilgallen.

A young Mary Pinchot Meyer.

Mary marries Cord Meyer, a war hero who lost an eye in a grenade attack in the Pacific. Later worked for the CIA.

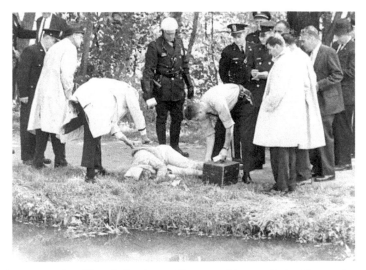

Police examine Mary's body on the canal towpath in Georgetown. Nobody has ever been convicted of her murder.

Florence Pritchett. *Flo*, as JFK called her was his long time lover and by all accounts great fun to be with. Also a close friend of Dorothy Kilgallen and appeared on her TV show. Only two days after Dorothy's death *Flow* was also found dead, Her autopsy reports cause of death *unknown*.

JFK in Navy uniform with Florence at the Stork Club, Feb 1944.

Florence Pritchett became Florence Smith when she married
Earl T. Smith, ambassador to Cuba.

Chapter 6 – The Last Dandy of Soho

Della slipped back behind the wheel before I got the chance to, saying: 'You know when Seb squeezed my arse?'

'Yeah, I wondered why you didn't charge him,'

'Very funny, well it still hurts from when your stupid nasty parrot bit me and there's a red mark the size of your fist.'

'Mickey', I said, 'is many things but never stupid.'

'That bird's dangerous and has put me out of business for the last week, he's cost me plenty.'

'What's this leading to Della? I gave you five hundred remember?'

'Well Darling…..'

Whenever she threw a "Darling" into the conversation I was on guard.

'I need the car for a few days. I've got some work down in south London with body makeup and low lighting. I can get away with my stage act as long as I don't dance too close to the guys in the front row.'

'OK bitch, but take care of it. Once you cross the river it gets wild down there, don't let them nick my new set of alloys. Do you want to come up for a quick one?' I asked as casually as I could manage.

'Would that be bar or bed or putting it plainly a quick drink or probably an even quicker screw?'

'A screw, naturally', I replied truthfully.

'No way am I stripping off in front of murderous Mickey. That will teach you to keep him in his cage.'

'I'll never do that. Would you like to live in a cage?'

'That's cute coming from a cage fighter.'

'Ex cage fighter and you can drop me off in Oxford Street, I'll walk the rest.' I watched the little Daihatsu pull away into the heavy traffic with that distinctive roar coming from the twin exhausts. Della still had the top down making her and the car look totally out of place amongst the black cabs and red double decker buses as rain started to fall.

I've always liked the rain. I find it clears the cobwebs out of my head. So while people rushed past me with umbrellas up I walked slowly back to my place, thinking hard about Zian and my progress with JFK.

Who or what the hell is Zian? OK, so he's a martial arts expert, highly intelligent, very well read about Western history and as charming and quietly spoken as he is, there's an almost military air about him, sort of authoritative, commanding. And Jia-Li, also trained in martial arts, very smart, very attractive. Is she really just a waitress in her Father's Chinese restaurant?

And what could this folder of Dorothy Kilgallen's contain? So she interviewed Jack Ruby. What in hells name

66

could he have told her that was so mind blowing, so dangerous, so powerful? So much so that a whole crowd of people who got close got taken out before they could talk. So he shot Lee Oswald. OK, that's big time enough but, in the general scheme of things, I would rate him as well down the list in the overall murder of JFK.

My being deep in thought came to an abrupt end as I turned into Hanway Street. The dark, quiet little street was a blaze of blue flashing lights from an ambulance plus two cop cars. My street door was open, paramedics were kneeling around someone on the floor. As I rushed forward a uniformed cop barred my way.

'I live here. I have the top floor flat', I said. Just then someone in the small crowd called out;

'Sure, if it isn't young Danny McQuade. He's a friend of Barney's.' It was Bridie Murphy, the Irish barmaid from the pub on the corner.

'OK', said the cop dropping his arm. To my horror Barney lay on the floor of his workshop, his face white as a ghost and his lips dark blue, his legs were shaking like hell. There was a large red, spreading blood stain on his shirt.

'Oh my God Barney, what's happened?' He reached up and stroked my face. The medic spoke very quietly.

'The old chap is very weak and can't speak. We've got to get him to hospital double quick.' Then a guy who I took to be a plain clothes cop with a strong Scots accent whispered in my ear.

'He's been shot at close range.'

'What!' I shouted. 'You can't be fucking serious? Who would want to hurt Barney? Who did this? Barney tell me, tell me? I'll tear the bastards apart!' The cop tried to pull me away.

'Get your hands off me', I warned him. Just then Barney touched my arm and raised his trembling hand pointing at the girl paramedic who was fixing a drip into his arm.

'No Barney, she's the ambulance lady, she's here to help you.' Then with his eyes almost closing he moved his fingers to the blood on his chest. 'When you bleed Barney it always looks worse than it is. Like when I get punched on the nose in the ring. Barney don't worry you're going to be OK. I'm coming with you.'

With that the medics lifted the stretcher into the ambulance. As they did so his fingers moved once more to the red first aid bag one of them was carrying. With that he let go of my hand with a final weak squeeze.

'What hospital are you taking him to?'

'Charing Cross', said the driver. Then they shut the back doors and the ambulance moved away fast, all blue lights and wailing sirens. I went back in and sat on the chair beside his sewing machine and cried like a baby. I just couldn't stop sobbing.

'I'm Detective Sergeant Mills.' It was the Scots guy again. He spoke quietly in a sympathetic, confiding way. 'There's never a good time to ask these questions but I'd really appreciate your help.'

'Yeah OK OK but be quick I've gotta get to the hospital.'

'Have you known Mr Goldman long?'

'Who? Oh Barney, yeah about four years.'

'Was he a man who made enemies?'

'No he never hurt a soul. All he had was his work that he loved. He made all my gear, he called me a clothes horse. Told me his wife died six years ago, they had no kids. Once a week he played cards with some old guys from his local Synagogue. Out the back of this workroom are a couple more rooms where he lived. That's about it.

'You live at the top of this block Mr McQuade, the fourth floor? Who lives in the two flats between the first and second floors?'

'No one, they're empty. The landlord hiked the rent so the people moved out. Me and Barney were planning to do the same.' Just then one of the uniform cops brought me in a mug of tea. I tried to pull myself together, wiping away my tears and taking long swigs of the hot tea.

'In Hell's name who'd want to hurt him?'

'Probably a robbery that went wrong', said Mills.

'But Barney was too old and frail to put up a fight and what is there to rob? He had nothing worth taking. Anyway, I'm off to Charing Cross and fast. I reached for my mobile to get Zian at the same time one of the cops came in and said something very quietly to Mills who then put his hand over mine to stop me dialling.

'It's just come over the patrol car radio.'

'What has?' I asked.

Speaking very softly he said. 'I'm very sorry to have to tell you your friend Barney has just died on the way to hospital.' I sat there for I don't know how long, too shocked to think straight.

After some time Mills asked very quietly, 'Are you all right Danny?'

'As alright as I'll ever be. Can I go now?'

'Sure, we are wrapping up now. The flat will be sealed off as a crime scene. It was most likely local punks high on drugs, we'll soon pick them up.'

'You'd better get to him first because if you don't I'll make sure he dies in agony.'

'It may not be a he Dan. Remember the female is deadlier than the male.' As I climbed the stairs I thought; *Copper, don't talk crap*.

Chapter 7 – Mickey Vs. Anita

I felt lonely, sad and depressed as I turned the key in my door. Mickey was on top of his cage fluffed up and head down.

'You've gotta right to be sulky Mickey boy. I've left you alone far too long this sad day'. He made no greeting, no Hello Dan, just moved his head in the direction of the living room. I came to with a jolt. He was telling me someone was here, couldn't be Della, she gave her key back. I tensed ready for action like when I step into the fighting cage ready for combat. I came slowly round the arch leading to my small living room and there she was.

Like a lightning flash in my head I knew this is what Barney had tried to tell me when he pointed to the girl paramedic and the red blood. Here she was facing me with her back to the French windows that open out onto my tiny narrow balcony, red coat, black mini skirt, blonde hair, a real stunner but a cold ice maiden holding a gun with what appeared to be a silencer pointed at my chest and only six feet away.

'What do you want?' I asked.

'What a stupid question McQuade.' She had an accent I couldn't place; 'I have come to kill you.'

'Why?' I asked, my voice sounding far away.

'I honestly don't know, but what I do know for sure is I'm being paid 75,000 Euros plus generous expenses.' Here I was facing death any second and I felt no fear, calm but totally alert.

'I must be really annoying someone very rich. Was poor old Barney annoying the same person?'

'No I called the other day to kill you and to bug your flat with this listening device', she quickly showed what looked like a tiny mobile. 'It's now disconnected of course, I don't want the sounds of your death sent over the air waves.'

She gave a cold smile as she slipped it back in her pocket and then continued. 'But you stayed out too long and when I left the old tailor man saw me and again tonight and so could identify me.'

'So you killed him?'

'Of course, I had to. Aren't you going to beg for your life McQuade? Most men do, more so than women.'

'But you still kill them?'

'Yes I do,' again that cold smile.

I knew the first bullets would hit me any second yet time seemed to stand still. Holding the gun firmly in her right hand she moved slowly around the back of my armchair and casually rested her left hand on top of Mickey's cage. Big mistake, with the speed of lightning he gave one of his ear shattering 120 decibel screeches and sank his huge vice-like beak into her fingers, like he would a snake in the Amazon rain forests. The intense pain and eardrum busting noise threw her off balance. All my years of fighting and training went into the next 30 seconds; my flying kick to her throat followed by a hard left jab to her guts, then a heavy right cross, my best punch, to her face. I heard the nose and cheek bones crack. She got off two shots; one went into the ceiling the other split the back of my old but comfy armchair. As the gun hit the floor I made a dive and grabbed it. Mickey was still hanging on to her hand, his wings beating fast at full span. Then, knowing he'd won the day, he flew up onto the curtain rail.

She staggered to the centre of the room sobbing and cursing in a foreign language. I could see that three of her fingers were almost severed, with her good hand she reached behind her collar and pulled out a long silver blade. Eyes mad with pain and fury she came at me like the enraged wounded animal she was. I fired twice hitting her right where the heart is. She reeled round mortally wounded, dropped the blade, stumbled crashing through the open French windows and ended up hanging over the low railings moaning.

I turned off the wall light, stepped out onto the dark balcony beside her. I looked across the street at the warehouse. All was quiet. No lights on, no one and nothing to be seen. Hoping she was still alive and could hear me I said;

'So you would have killed me? You killed my dear old pal Barney, and done me out of a vicuna sports jacket! The first two with time, a hell of a lot of time, I could maybe just maybe forgive. But the vicuna sports jacket never!'

She gave a low moan. 'I guess you know the old saying bitch; *No one ever dies happy*' With that I took hold of her ankles and tipped her over, red coat swirling like a parachute she spiralled down four floors and hit the concrete with a sickening thud. She then lay motionless in the little courtyard of Barney's back basement.

As my building was now empty except for me, no one would see her until the police came again tomorrow to check Barney's flat for clues. I stepped back in, closing the doors behind me. Mickey was back on top of his cage eating a piece of banana like nothing had happened.

'Della's right Mickey, you belong in the jungle, but I'm sure glad you were here tonight.' He looked up and gave a contented squawk.

'Hi Zian I know it's late. If I promise not to swear can you call round right now, I'm in very big trouble, real big.' I heard him say something to somebody in Chinese before he replied.

'Where are you Mr Dan?' He sounded surprised almost shocked.

'I'm at my flat. Where else would I be?'

'But your car is down in South East London.'

'I know, I lent it to Della, she had a gig down there.'

'Are you alone?'

'Yes I am now.'

'Mr Dan I be round at once. Look out of window before you come downstairs and open door, to make sure it is me OK?'

'I'll do that. Hey Zian how the hell did you know where my car was?' Too late, he'd hung up. As I replaced the phone I noticed my hand was shaking like a leaf, guess that's what they call aftershock.

In one evening I'd spent an hour or so with a very strange but likeable guy who calls himself the "Dandy of the Underworld", lost a dear old pal due to gun shot wounds, came within a split second of being killed by a vicious lady assassin who'd been paid a lot of money to make me dead, only to be saved by an equally vicious pet Macaw. How many people can say they owe their life to a large parrot? Then to round off a pleasant day I get revenge by tipping the lady over my balcony to her death. I'm starting to really enjoy being a writer, where else could you get this sort of buzz? Fighting in the ring or cage doesn't even come close.

I went once more onto the balcony and looked down at the basement. Nothing had changed, she still lay there, the moonlight shining on her blonde hair. Then to my horror

I noticed Mickey sitting a couple of feet away from me, his large claws gripping the balcony railing, silently staring out into the darkness. With all the madness going on I'd forgotten that I'd left the French window doors open behind me, I tried to coax him back in. 'Don't leave me Mickey. You wouldn't survive out there it's cold and dark, no cashew nuts or red peppers.' He tilted his head toward me listening then stretched his wings full span and took off. I yelled his name. He circled once then landed on the roof of the warehouse across the street; I called again at the top of my voice. He looked over at me. There was almost a silent understanding between us, like we both knew it was his instinct to be free. He took off again faster this time flying high and fast heading South towards the river. I watched heartbroken until the tiny dot that was my pal disappeared from sight.

I came in, flopped in the armchair and cried long and hard for the second time this sad and lonely night.

Chapter 8 – Stumblebums And Cardboard Cut-Outs

I walked through to my bedroom that looks out on the street, all was quiet, just the odd cab passing. Then a black Chrysler 300C, with only its side lights on, pulled round the corner and stopped outside. Four guys got out closing the car doors very quietly.

Zian looked up at me, I went down the stairs two at a time to open the door. He greeted me in what, for him, was an almost emotional way. Gripping my shoulders he said, 'I am so glad you are OK Mr Dan. I make very bad mistake. I put my friend's life at risk through my stupidity.'

'I don't know what you're going on about Zian but first hear what I've got to tell you and listen good.' I looked at the three other Chinese guys. They looked real cool and heavy, like Zian they all wore smart suits. I was used to seeing Zian in a leather jacket.

'It is OK Mr Dan you can say anything in front of my men, we are as one.'

'I'll never get into a rickshaw again without wondering who the hell is really peddling me', I said. We sat down and I told him all that had happened; Barney and the girl who tried to kill me, and how I'd lost Mickey. 'Would you guys like a drink?' I asked

'No' said Zian. 'We are on duty.'

'You sound like the police.'

'In a way we are.'

'Well I'll have one.' I poured a double whisky. I took a large gulp, letting it hit the back of my throat.

'Man that's good, I needed that.' Zian smiled and continued;

'First I am sorry to hear about your two friends: the old tailor gentleman and your beloved bird. *The same force formed the sparrow that fashioned man the King. The God of the whole gave a spark of soul. To furred and to feathered thing.*'

'OK Zian I'll buy it, who said that?'

'Ella Wheeler Wilcox, she animal lover like you. She American lady poet.'

'Sounds cool, I'd like to meet her.'

'Too late Mr Dan she die 1920. You say he headed for the river, those birds can fly hundreds of miles as they do in the rain forests. He will cross the river Thames and head for the South coast then cross the channel, that is only seventy miles away, then on into France.'

'Why would he do that?' I asked.

'He is seeking the warmer weather that is in his soul. He will find it the closer he gets to the Mediterranean.'

Oh God I hope so, I thought to myself, the thought of him out in the cold London night air broke my heart.

Zian, followed by his men, walked out onto the balcony. They looked over for a few minutes then he turned and spoke in Chinese to the other men in a firm voice like he was giving orders. They left the room and hurried down the stairs.

'Before you ask how I knew where your car was I will try to explain Mr Dan.'

'Yeah I'd like that and I'll try not to swear.' He sat down again.

'The lady down there is Anita Harga, also known as Amelia Larsson. She is professional assassin. She has killed over twenty people this year, three of them my people. She is in the top four hit men, or in this case women, in the World. This year she has killed in the USA, Germany, France, and in the UAE. She is, or thanks to you was, a Swedish citizen living in a town called Malmo. My men are right now getting rid of the body. The police when they call tomorrow will find no trace of her ever being here. You recall I told you I was collecting a fare in my rickshaw from a hotel in The Strand and taking her to the American embassy?'

'Yeah I do, I said *I hope she wouldn't be too heavy.*'

'Yes Mr Dan, well that was her. The reason I did that was to put a trace on her. We wanted to know where she went and why she was here. On the seat of my rickshaw was a tiny tracking device the size of a grain of rice. When she sat down it stuck to coat, she never knew it was there. I also had one fitted to your little sports car, I made the mistake of assuming where the car was so you too.

'So you knew she was here but thought I was down South London way.'

'Yes and when you headed back I would of course have intercepted you before you get here. Our embassy in San Francisco told us she had left Sweden and she only leaves Sweden on killing mission. She very clever at one time we lost her, she came a roundabout route through Europe by coach then ferry, across channel then train to London using different names all the way. She never fly direct.'

'OK tell me why she was going to the American embassy.'

'We are not sure yet but it was unofficial, that is to say she meeting an individual privately.'

'And when she got there someone told her to kill me?'

'Yes my friend, correct.'

'But that's crazy, what the hell for?'

'Because of the book you are writing, you are worrying the power elite.'

'For fuck's sake Zian, I haven't come up with anything yet.'

'Please Mr Dan you're swearing again. Anyway, your lady assassin told me even she didn't know the reason. She tells truth, she not interested in reasons, only the fee she being paid. Now my friend thanks to you she never enjoy spending it.' He gave a satisfied smile.

'Tell me Zian, way back when we first met, was that meeting just chance?'

'No I planned it because I knew you would lead me to something but as I got to know you I realise I like you very much, you honourable man. You half gentleman half savage. I proud now that you call me friend.'

'Zian there are thousands of books out there on the JFK killing. All those authors never had any trouble, why me?'

'You wrong, many had plenty big trouble, but I think by chance you approach subject from a totally new and very unusual angle; via Kilgallen the journalist and Ray the singer. The power elite know that you could get dangerously close to the reason the President and so many other people were murdered. So they think better to stop you now before too late. Tonight you are tired my friend, lock up your flat it is unhappy place for you. Be my guest, stay at the Chinese embassy I have small apartment there.' A rickshaw driver with a flat at the embassy, you gotta be kidding.

I felt too tired, not to mention confused, to argue so quickly packed a bag and followed Zian down the stairs. As I passed Barney's door I noticed it was covered with yellow tape saying *police crime scene do not enter*.

'You car crazy so you drive', said Zian as he tossed me the keys. 'You like?' He asked as I got behind the wheel of the 310C.

'You bet I do, sure beats that rickshaw.'

'This one V8 six litre 0 to 60 in 5 seconds.'

'Yeah just what you need if assassins are after you, but I still prefer my little two seater.' As we pulled out into Oxford Street I said. 'Your embassy is in Kensington like all the others right?'

'No Mr Dan, it's up top of Regents Street past BBC and into Portland Place.'

'Trust you to be different Zian.'

He laughed saying, 'Tomorrow we talk. I explain many things to you.'

'I look forward to that pal and I promise I'll hold back on the swearing.'

My room at the embassy was luxurious. Feeling exhausted I lay in until about 10am then met Zian for a brief tour of the place.

'We are completely self-contained here', he said, waving his hands about like a tour guide. 'Our own power supply and water system and armoury. We even have our own medical section with operating theatre.'

I noticed everyone treated him with great respect, I resisted asking him again who he really is; let him tell me if he wants to. I discreetly handed him a small bag that I'd brought with me from the flat.

'What's this Mr Dan?'

'I picked them up before you and your men arrived. They belonged to Blondie.'

He took a quick look inside then said 'Let's go to the armoury.' Once there he took out the tiny transmitter and then the long knitting needle type blade. 'You were so lucky my friend,' he said holding it carefully by the small handle. 'It is designed to release a shot of cyanide once it enters the body.' I thought to myself; *thanks again Mickey wherever you are.*

Zian looked at the gun with an expert eye, he obviously knew about them. 'This is a Browning Hi Power 9mm with fitted silencer, at that range it would have punched hole right through you. I'll keep these Mr Dan and I have one for you.' He went over to a metal wall cabinet and came back with a small revolver.

'Zian, I don't have a licence. If I'm caught with that I'll get five years. Anyway the only gun I've ever fired, except for last night, is an air rifle at a fairground!'

Ignoring what I said, he continued, 'This is a Smith & Wesson 36 caliber, but it been specially adapted by us; it now has the punch and range of a much bigger gun. It is fully loaded and here are two spare clips of ammo, they all fit in this small bag that will fix by Velcro inside your coat. If the police do catch you with it I have enough diplomatic clout to free you within hour.'

'In that case I'll try knocking over my local bank.' He gave one of his quick smiles, then put ear protectors on and gave me a set. For the next hour he taught me how to hold the gun, reload fast and fire at targets up close and 75 yards away. He had his own gun; a Walther P38 and he never missed.

'I'm starting to feel like John Wayne in the Wild West, Zian.'

'This more dangerous my friend. This the Wild West End of London.' Later we sat facing each other in his room in deep gold leather armchairs while a very pretty waitress served tea.

'I could get used to this Zian', he gave another of his rare smiles.

'I don't think so my friend, you're too wild in your heart, all this would suffocate you.'

'Before you begin Zian can I ask one question?' Before he could answer I said, 'Last night you mentioned that I was worrying the power elite in case I got too close to the truth about JFK. Who the hell are they?'

Looking very serious he asked the waitress to bring a large writing pad. She did and then he took from his top pocket and handed me an expensive gold fountain pen. 'As I explain Mr Dan, you can make notes for book.'

Looking at the pen I said, 'Zian you've sure got style. But as a back up I'll also use this.' I clicked on my small recorder and placed it beside me.

'The power elite', he continued 'are the most powerful people on earth. Quite simply they run Western World and have done for over three centuries.' He said it like *doesn't every school kid know that*!

'If the people who really rule and control this country and entire Western World, including the USA, came into this room you would not recognise them, their names and faces would mean nothing to you. All these Prime Ministers and Presidents that are paraded in front of you every day on your TV screens are mere stumble bums and cardboard cut-outs. Sure they're important people and make big decisions but no way do they hold real power. The present power structure started around 1910. A group of all powerful bankers got together in Washington DC to take control of World finances; the Rothschild's, the Rockefellers, Astor's, J.P.Morgan, Warburg's, Kuhn & Loeb, along with the Bank of England and the British and German Royal families and in

1913 they set up Federal Reserve Bank. In other words a World bank.

It's very name is a complete and utter deception, it sounds like the USA's Government bank but it is, in fact, like Bank of England, a private bank; it hides behind a mass of economic gibberish to fool the people of the Western World. When the First World War was started by them only a year later in 1914 those bankers were financing both sides, and making massive loans to every country involved. Britain, for example, was still paying off interest on its loans when the Second World War started in 1939.

The Tsar of Russia was the only one who refused to go along with their plans, so they financed the Russian revolution, and when the Tsar was captured by the Communists your King George V and the German Kaiser, who were all cousins, could have saved the Tsar and his family but refused an offer by the Japanese to rescue him and turned down his plea to come and live in England. So when he was murdered they carved up his incredible fortune. Lenin and the communists got the land and palaces, but he had four-hundred million dollars invested in American banks alone plus huge amounts of cash and priceless jewellery in London and Zurich, the power elite got their hands on that.

They consist of only two hundred or so members at any one time. Today it is mainly of course the International

Bankers, but a few oil people, vast land owners, politicians and Royalty. They can start and stop wars when it suits them, they can bankrupt countries and huge multi nationals, or save them. Why for example do you think your flat goes up every year in value then, for no discernable reason, crashes to quarter of its value overnight?'

'I don't own my flat, it's rented.' He carried on like he hadn't heard me.

'In the early 1960s they decided on a New World Order. They were in a position now to rule the World with an iron fist. First they needed JFK to go along with their plans but he refused point blank. Not only that but him and his brother Robert, the Attorney General, were about to expose them. And just four months before they murdered him he issued Executive Order Number 11110.

Chapter 9 – Executive Order Number 11110

'Some time before his death he made speech saying that secret societies were taking over America and he promised the people he would not let this happen, and that he would stop the Vietnam war and bring home the troops within next year. That of course would have cost the industrial military complex, who are funded by the World Bank, billions and billions of dollars. Then just for good measure he said he intended breaking up and dismantling the CIA and the FBI.'

'That must have pleased J Edgar Hoover no end Zian?'

'Making that speech and issuing order 11110 was his greatest mistake. He may as well have issued his own death warrant. They decided he had to be eliminated.

He was only 46 when killed in '63 so born 1917, the year of Snake. Those people have good temper and are very skilful in communicating.'

As the waitress poured us more tea I asked him what this executive order was, and why such a big deal?

'With that order he would at one stroke have put the Federal Reserve Bank out of business and made the USA Treasury department the only rightful power to make and issue currency and most importantly it would be debt free currency, this new money would be backed by silver. But Federal Reserve money is not backed by anything.'

'What exactly did their New World Order entail Zian?'

'Have you ever read George Orwell's 1984 Mr Dan?'

'Yes I have, and seen the movie, terrifying.'

'Well what they have in mind is 1984 magnified by fifty. They have succeeded already in many respects. Take UK, you have more CCTV cameras than any other country on earth. You are watched and spied upon from when you leave home until you return. On average in UK you are caught on camera over 100 times a day, and before long you will have cameras inside your home as well.'

'Yeah, but from what I've heard your China ain't exactly a Democracy.'

'Mr Dan, you think you're living in a Democracy because every five years you put a cross on a piece of paper? That Channel Tunnel wasn't built for you to have a holiday in Paris. It is for rapid troop movement and compulsory transportation of workers to whatever part of Europe they are needed, all types of hellish things are in store for the people of the West. Euthanasia for the old and disabled, long term conscription, forced military service for men and women, medical help only for key workers. Severe restrictions on travel; you will need permits to go just a few miles from your home. And a total break up of the family unit as you know it.

You, for example, as a young man will serve five years hard military service and then maybe be sent to Russia or Eastern Europe to work for many years. Holidays, fancy clothes or owning your home and car will, for the masses, be a thing of the past. Take for example *Political Correctness,* its real name is *Social Marxism*. Who do you think inflicted that on the people? A few years ago no one had even heard the expression, now people in UK dare not say anything in case it is not PC.'

'How did Kilgallen find out about this future hell on earth?'

'We are not sure but she had close contacts in the White House and of course with Jack Ruby. She knew about Executive order 11110 and got her hands on the original copy of the New World Order and was killed because of that.'

'But what became of it, that's the million dollar question?'

'Now with the advantage of nearly fifty years hindsight it looks as though she did send it to her singer lover Johnnie Ray. At the time no one would have suspected him, she was very clever in doing that but what the hell did he do with it? Don't be misled about him using it to help the cause of Gay rights, that's a red fish.'

'A red what Zian?'

'My English not good Mr Dan, what is it that I mean?'

'I think you mean *red herring* and for the record your English is better than mine.' As we finished our tea, I thought to myself; *your English is just maybe too good, at times at least*, before continuing; 'I guess that Ray the singer read it and realised just what he had gotten into and it scared the hell out of him.'

'No I forgot to mention Mr Dan, he maybe could not read it all because we think it might be written mostly in code.'

'So Kilgallen couldn't read it all either?'

'Possibly someone broke the code for her because she knew the meaning and content of it, she knew the sheer power of that document.'

I continued writing down my notes as fast as possible with Zian's smooth fountain pen, and my voice recorder on the table getting every word we spoke.

Zian continued, 'You see everyone involved in JFK's death only knew their own small part, no one except the power elite knew the whole plan. There were members of the Mafia the CIA, FBI and Free Masons involved. They were offered massive sums of money in advance to play their small part, but even they did not really know who their pay masters were. Ruby's job was to take out Oswald before they got him into court and he could talk. Ruby was told two million dollars would be waiting for him on release from prison and Americas top lawyers would make sure he would only get 3 years, and be out in two. It went badly wrong. He got the death sentence, then he got scared and mad.'

'That's a dangerous combination Zian.'

'Too true, so he decided to talk. That's when he asked to see Dorothy Kilgallen. If you're going to talk then talk to the best and Dorothy had a Worldwide audience. Ruby was later killed in prison; he was injected with cancer cells. Oswald did not fire the fatal shot, that came from a sharpshooter on the underpass who hit JKF in the throat. Note in the movie of the killing how JFK's hand goes up to his throat and his head jolts back.'

'Yeah, my publisher gave me the DVD but I haven't had time to watch it yet.'

'Well you will see he was shot from the front; the massive damage at the back of his head is an exit wound. Take the parade itself; JFK is travelling in a new Lincoln convertible at 8 mph followed by two 5 year old Cadillac convertibles full of, as it turned out, totally useless secret service men. The drivers were told to keep a distance of only 6 to 8 feet between each car.

Emory Roberts, a very suspect person, was the head man in charge of that secret service group and was travelling in the car behind JFK. Back at the airport at the start of the motorcade he gave an order to leave off the hard thick clear plastic bubble top that fitted like a roof over the car and would have given the occupants some protection. The day before he over ruled the Dallas Police Department who rightly said they should be guarding the President. Texas Rangers would have been carrying sub machine guns instead of the useless hand guns Roberts and his bunch of clowns carried but never used.

And how about this Mr Dan, as the cars turned into Dealey Plaza, Roberts ordered his two men who were standing on a special platform on the rear of the Lincoln to stand down! So giving the assassins a clear line of fire. If those two men had been in place they would not only have blocked the assassins view from the book warehouse but thrown themselves over JFK to protect him as soon as they heard the first shot that did come from behind but missed, the second shot hit home.'

'I assume, Zian, that was fired by Oswald?'

'You assume wrong Mr Dan. The killer in the school book warehouse was a man named Mac Wallace, a known hit man with strong links to the Mafia and friend of Lyndon Baines Johnson, the US Vice President; the Mafia bosses at that time being Carlos Marcello, Santos Trafficante, Johnny Roselli and Sam Giancana.

JFK was killed in a classic military style triangular ambush. A lone marksman in the school book warehouse Wallace, not Oswald. Looking from the front he was behind JFK to his left, he hit JFK in the back. To his right another marksman, Giancana's bodyguard Richard Cain in the

County Records Building, hit Governor John Connally by mistake. His orders were to take out Jackie Kennedy. Finally, in front to the Presidents front up on the grassy knoll...'

'Hold on Zian. I heard this knoll thing before, what the hell is a knoll?'

'An American term, Mr Dan. It means a small sloping grass hill or bank with trees.'

'Right, OK, carry on.'

'That is where the real killer was placed. He had the perfect view of the motorcade coming towards him, he couldn't miss and he didn't. This one we are not sure about but believe he was an international killer with the code name "Saul". Born in France and served in the French foreign legion but had lived in America since the mid 1950's. He was also a master of disguise, hence the man in police uniform seen carrying a rifle behind the fence at the top of the knoll. Each marksman had a back up man to get him away fast, there was a team of 6 expert killers in Dealey Plaza that day.

Saul's backup man was almost certainly Charles Nicolletti, top contract killer for the Mafia. Oswald was in the building but he was planted there as a fall guy or, as he said himself, 'just a patsy'. And that is what he became, the pathetic misguided fool. Kill the President? He couldn't even drive a car!

Within 18 months of JFK's death over 300 people closely connected with his murder, or witnesses, or maybe those who knew too much about some aspect of it, were murdered themselves or lets say died in very suspicious circumstances. Johnny Roselli was choked to death, his body then cut up and put in an oil drum that was found floating off the Florida coast. This happened while he was under close police protection because he had been subpoenaed to testify about what he knew relating to the murder of JFK.'

'Don't be too hard on the cops, Zian. They were probably busy giving out parking tickets.' Not for the first time he ignored my quick fire humour and continued.

'Sam Giancana got a bullet in the back of the head then five shots around the mouth, a warning that he talked too much.

Richard Cain also got murdered gangland style. He was in a restaurant when four men came in wearing ski masks and carrying shotguns. They put him against the wall and blew his head off.

Wallace crashed his car; the car's exhaust had been fixed to slowly release carbon monoxide into the car sending Wallace unconscious while driving. He died of massive head injuries.

Nicoletti was also due to give evidence regarding what he knew about the JFK murder but never turned up due to someone firing three bullets into the back of his head!'

Chapter 10 – The West Is In Trouble

'Zian, this is all hugely fascinating stuff but, OK so you get your hands on this document spelling out the New World Order, about what the bastards have got planned for us and how it's the world bankers who really run things, and it was them who killed JFK and later his brother and fuck knows how many others since 1963. So what are you or China going to do with it?'

He made a face like he was in pain, maybe because I swore. Then he raised his hand beckoning the lovely waitress over, 'A drink Mr Dan?'

'Yeah thanks, double whisky no ice.'

He said something in Chinese to her and she was gone, then he rested his head on the back of his plush chair and closed his eyes as if meditating. Gorgeous came back and handed me my drink with a dazzling smile, I smiled back and winked. She then put Zian's drink on the table in front of him. He opened his eyes. Do not flirt with the waitress my young friend, she does not speak a word of English.'

'So what? I don't speak Chinese.'

'Mr Dan I will try and make it as simple as possible.'

'Yeah do that because I'm getting writer's cramp', I replied and started making notes once more as fast as I could.

'The West is in terrible trouble.' He said it slowly with his eyes closed again and a very sad look on his face. 'America as a world power is starting to fall apart and is, thanks to the Federal Reserve Bank, deeply in debt. It is also torn apart by internal strife. Remember the planes that smashed into the World Trade towers took off from American airfields. So to appease their enemies the Liberal Power Elite put in place a new President that up to a week before no one had heard of. His full name is Barak Hussein Obama?'

'Yeah but you know Zian, I really liked that Sarah Palin, what a President she would make. Imagine what Clinton would do with her in the Oval Office, Monica Lewinsky wouldn't get a look in, but enough of my sexual fantasies.'

He ignored my quick fire humour again and continued. 'But it will not and is not working. America's best friend, the UK, is also spending vast sums of money abroad while the people on the street get poorer by the day. Worse still, as I have said, the UK is now a surveillance society rigidly controlled by the media and a very corrupt and perverse judiciary and legal system. Your once noble police force has been undermined from the top by political correctness.

The City of London, the financial heart of the UK has far more power than the politicians in Westminster who have lost all their independence to Brussels and the Euro Government. The USA and Europe also have to face the terrifying fact that Iran, Saudi Arabia, Egypt, and Turkey are now nuclear powers. The USA and UK now resemble dangerous lost and wounded animals, and will try anything to divert their people's anger, by starting more foreign wars.

They see China as a super power, not involved in their self-made disasters. We are now overtaking the USA as the World's fastest growing economy. This will be the Chinese century but we have no quarrel with anyone, no one has the man power we have. Every third person in the world is Chinese, we are almost self-sufficient. But should the wounded animal of the West lash out in panic at us in the East, that folder revealing the horrors they have in store for their own people would be the most powerful weapon for us to have up our sleeve. If we threatened to make the contents of that folder public all hell would break loose on the streets of the USA and the UK leading to civil war. So as long as they know we have it we can keep them in check and make them think twice before starting some irreversible global disaster. That is why they are so desperate to get it back, and why we are so keen to have it.' He finished of course with an irritating quote '*First they ignore you, then they ridicule you, then they fight you, then you win.*'

'Don't tell me that was Confucius' wife?'

'No, leader of India Mahatma Gandhi, he too assassinated in 1948.'

He sank back into his chair looking serious as though he had just revealed to me some enormous world super plan, which in a way I guess he had. I really like the guy so didn't want to hurt his feelings but knew what I was about to say would do just that.

'Zian, I think you or your country have got it wrong.' He looked surprised and shocked. 'I go along with all you say about the World banks, it makes sense. I never did go along with that main line crap. Hey listen everyone, it was just a lone *nutter* called Lee Oswald, or that it was the Mafia who killed JFK because the bottom line is they're just a bunch of gangsters. They couldn't pull something off as big as that. Some of them were involved, sure, along with the CIA, FBI and others. But only a super powerful force like International bankers could attempt it and fund it. Only they too would have the essential insiders giving them the go ahead from the White House.

But I have to tell you you're wrong about the reactions of the man in the street. Forget uprisings and riots, the army crushing the police and then siding with the people, it ain't never going to happen. In the 50s or 60s maybe, but not today. The Brits have had over forty years of being dumbed down, by the education system and the media, the powers that be who run everything know that for sure.'

I got up and went over to the bay window and looked out on the busy street. 'See that guy over there Zian?' He twisted round in his chair to follow where I was pointing. 'That guy in the T-Shirt and shabby jeans standing at the bus stop.'

'Yes I see Mr Dan.'

'Well he's around 35, he's got a shaven head and tattoos all over his head and arms, a stud through his nose and ears, probably one through his tongue as well. On his feet are worn down trainers, when new they were white, now they're dirty grey. You could tell him and millions like him what the evil bastards have ready for him and his family and you know what Zian? He wouldn't give a shit. Mind you if you closed down the football club he supports or banned some stupid 'Soap' or reality TV show he watches every night, then you could have a revolution on your hands.'

Zian shook his head slowly. 'I have more respect for your people than you Mr Dan.'

'But I know them better than you Zian. I was born here in London. I'm not educated like you but I'm street wise. I guess you come from the upper class in China, been to Universities, lived in the States, and now you live here in this embassy that's on a level with Buckingham Palace. So don't tell me about the modern day people in the UK, I'm one of them, you're not. You have a picture of them in your mind that's out of date and wrong.

Before my last fight I had just fifteen quid in my pocket and stuck a *For Sale* notice in my car window. I won that fight so hung onto my car. I'm finished as a fighter so if Bob Appleby don't like this book I'm working on I'm back on Shit Street again. But when you wrap up here in London you'll fly first class back to Shanghai where no doubt you have a luxury apartment.'

A long silence followed then he said:

'Yes I do have a very nice apartment near the *Tomorrow Building* but your words have hurt me Mr Dan.'

'Well the truth does that Zian. I'll see ya. Oh by the way, sorry I swore.'

JFK welcomes a delegation of Creek Indians to the White House.

The Kennedy Brothers. Left to right; John, Robert and Edward.

JFK with singer and movie star Frank Sinatra.

JFK with Russian leader Nikita Khrushchev in Vienna, June 1961. When news of JFK's death reached the Kremlin Khrushchev broke down calling it a "Heinous Crime". The Russians were very quick to assure the USA that the Soviet Union had nothing to do with the death of their President.

JFK tries to restrain his Vice-President Lyndon
Johnson as he turns to threaten someone in the crowd.

Left to right; JFK (President), J. Edgar Hoover (Head of
the FBI) and Robert Kennedy (Attorney General), in the Oval Office at
the White House.

JFK takes questions at a White House press conference.

JFK with Jackie arriving at Dallas airport Love Field just after 11am on Friday 22nd November 1963. An hour and a half later he was dead.

A few minutes from death JFK smiles and waves at the crowd. The bodyguards' Cadillac stays close as do the motorcycle outriders, but the two special bodyguards are not on the Lincoln's rear platform. They have been ordered to stand down.

JFK's car turns into Dealey Plaza. In 30 seconds time the World would change forever. The time is 12.30pm (Central Time)

Lyndon Baines Johnson is sworn in as the new president. Jackie stands beside him still wearing her coat covered with the President's blood.

Lee Oswald being led out of the Dallas Police H.Q via the basement. No one appears to notice Jack Ruby, gun in hand, moving in fast from the right.

2 seconds later he presses his gun against Oswald and fires. A cop in a light suit jumps back in shock.

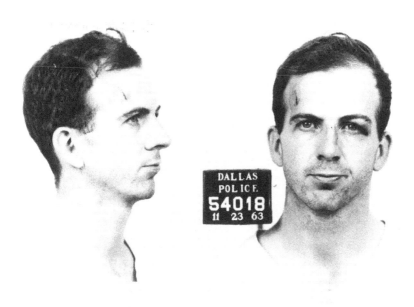

Mug shot of Lee Harvey Oswald.

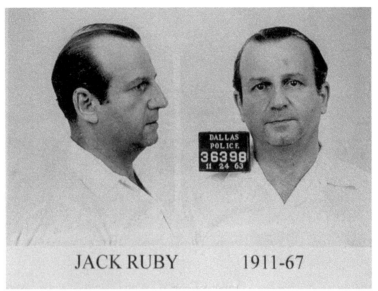

JACK RUBY   1911-67

Mug shot of Jack Ruby, the killer of Lee Harvey Oswald.

Club owner Jack Ruby with some of the girls from his Carousel Club.

June 5th1968, Ambassador Hotel, Los Angeles. Robert Kennedy states he is running for President. Soon after this picture was taken he is assassinated by (like his brother) gunshots to the head.

Barack Hussein Obama, the 44th and current President of the United States.

Chapter 11 – Look Homeward Angel

As I cut back towards Oxford Street my mobile rang, 'Hello dear boy.' It was Seb Horsley. 'Did you think I had forgotten you?'

'I know you'd never do that Seb because you're in love with me.' He gave that infectious half laugh half giggle.

'Well slightly in love dear boy, let's not exaggerate. But you were adorable in your last fight. That beast kept punching you to the floor, and every time he did I loved the way you tried to get back on your feet.'

'The bottom line Seb is, I lost.'

'Yes darling, but magnificently. Now to business, you know you asked me all about that Johnnie Ray stuff. Well we've had a marvellous bit of luck, can you call round?'

'Sure, I'm not far away. I'll be there before you put the phone down.' Seb was standing at his street door.

'Come in dear boy; wait 'til you hear all this.' I'd never seen him so excited, and with his excitable nature that's saying something. 'I don't know where to begin Danny; I have this dear friend, a very high ranking diplomat at the American embassy. When I first came to London years ago, we were an item.' He paused and a warm smile crossed his handsome face as he recalled some long ago happy memory.

'He is very elderly now but way way back in the 1950's he was a young fan of Johnnie Ray's, this is when he lived in LA. They all went around together, he told me every night was party night at Ray's place. I think they became an item for a while and Ray confided in him.'

'So Ray was gay?'

'Well once the love of his life, Dorothy Kilgallen, had been murdered I guess he reverted back to the *Gay Scene*.'

'And did he have anything to bribe the US Government with to get gays a better deal Seb?'

'No, not according to Guy Freeman, that's my friend at the embassy. All that stuff people have talked about for years about gays having some sort of secret information to beat the US Government over the head with and demand gay rights never happened. It was just that times, as they do, changed. But there is much more serious stuff that did happen.

In 1989 Ray sent Guy a painting of himself in his super star days. The title of the painting was *Look Homeward Angel,* named after one of his hit numbers. With it was a short message saying; g*uard this picture with your life Guy, it contains a plan for a living hell for those to come*. Well Guy couldn't make sense of it so phoned Johnnie to thank him and ask about the strange note. Johnnie told him he was planning to come over to London very soon when he would explain all, but no way could he talk on the phone. So Guy thought it all very odd, but then suddenly in February 1990 Johnnie died in LA.

The painting was done originally by London artist Mike Shaw, a fabulous artist. Being an artist myself I know Mike. He's been here in Soho for years painting portraits of celebs. He's a pal of your boss Bob Appleby who has a website of Mike's work and Bob is going to display some of my shark pictures.'

'I didn't know that, Seb. I assumed he was just into publishing.'

'No, your Bob is a man of many parts Dan. Well Guy had the portrait for years and just recently asked Mike if he would do a retouch where the sunlight had caused it to fade and reframe it. Now when Guy opened up the old frame to take out the painting there was a large heavy card envelope taped to the back of the painting marked *Top Secret*. It was sub-titled: *Outline of basic plans for NWO (New World Order) - These documents must not leave the Presidential Office*.

Well Guy read it and was stunned. He said to me poor JR must have carried this burden all those years since Dorothy Kilgallen got murdered.' Seb paused for effect and lay back on his small settee dramatically waiting for my reaction, and he got one.

'How the hell did you come by all this Seb?'

'Don't shout darling. Listen, I bumped into Mike at the club and he told me he was looking for a new studio because his lousy landlord had trebled the rent and did I know of anywhere. Then we got talking about art, and he told me he had just completed some artwork; a portrait of Johnnie Ray for my pal Guy. So of course when I heard that name he had my undivided attention.'

'When did all this take place Seb?'

'I think he returned the finished portrait of Ray back to Guy less than a week ago.'

'Did Mike the artist know anything about the envelope?'

'No nothing. Since then your boss Bob has purchased the Ray portrait from Guy and put it on his Stagedoor website, and of course Bob knows nothing about the envelope either.'

'So as we speak Seb, the envelope is with your pal at the US embassy, where it's been hanging on a wall for years without him knowing what was hidden in the frame?'

'Well yes and no dear boy. Guy is on his way here by taxi as we speak with the envelope.'

'You're not serious Seb?'

'I am indeed my lovely Dan. Dan the fighter man.' My mind went into overdrive then stalled in confusion as I tried to piece together how I'd arrived at this place. Seb put a large brandy and coke in my hand that I knocked back in a daze, he then handed me another, this time a large rum and black.

There was a soft knock on the street door. Seb greeted an old man warmly with a hug and a kiss on both cheeks. 'Dan this is my friend of many years Guy Freeman, US Diplomat. Guy meet Dan McQuade the boxer and cage fighter.'

'Real pleased to meet you Mr McQuade.' He was tall, well dressed and had an elegant old World charm about him, Southern charm by the sound of his Deep South accent. 'I have told Sebastian many times he need not reveal a persons employment when introducing them.' We all laughed, so breaking the ice.

'I have seen you in the ring and on TV. You took a bad beating in your last fight, are you fully recovered?'

'Yes I'm fine. I hope my fighter days are past now. I'm working on my first book that I believe Seb has told you about.'

'Yes indeed he has, may I call you Dan?'

'Sure, please do.'

He opened a small briefcase and took out an old worn looking large padded envelope that, at a guess, was slightly bigger than A4 size and maybe two inches thick. I could see the words "Top Secret" in large letters. I could also see it had been sealed with wide tape on the back.

'This, Dan, is what President John F. Kennedy, his brother Attorney General Robert Kennedy, Dorothy Kilgallen, and her husband, Richard Kollmar, Florence Smith, Mary Meyer, Marie Eichler, and so many many other brave souls were murdered for.'

'So Guy this tells us who killed JFK?'

'Not exactly, maybe in a way even more important than that, it tells us why he and the others were killed.'

'I thought I'd try my luck and asked 'Would this be to do with a New World Order?'

'How in God's name did you know that Dan?'

'I didn't, call it an educated guess', I lied.

The old man looked shocked, Seb made a timely step in saying 'Guy, Dan, what will you have?'

'I'll have a whiskey, make it large.' I replied.

Seb gave me a wink and said 'OK Dan, and I'll join you, what about you Guy?'

'No thanks my doctor won't let me. I regret to say I take too many drugs.'

'So do I, mainly cocaine', said Seb with a big grin.

Guy looked sad saying, 'I know you do and I wish you didn't but in my case they are medical drugs for my many illnesses.'

'Are you ill Guy?' I asked tactlessly.

He smiled at me and I suddenly felt close to this likeable gracious old man. We were separated by generations, countries, culture, and sexual preferences, and yet I knew we were on the same wavelength. I like or dislike people within five minutes of meeting them. This one I liked.

'Yes Dan, I have heart trouble and I am diabetic, but my main illness is I'm eighty four and tired of life. When I wake in the morning I'm cross that I have to face another day. And all my old friends have gone before me, and I have no family.'

'Oh come on Guy what about me?' said Seb in a hurt tone of voice.

'We were once lovers Seb so of course we are still the best of friends but you worry me; you're so dangerous to yourself. Promise me Dan you will look out for my crazy pal, don't let him be crucified again.'

'I promise Guy. If he does I'll climb up and pull the nails out with my teeth.' We all broke up laughing. 'Where do you hail from Guy?' I asked.

'I came from poor folks in Savannah Georgia. When I dream at night I'm back there and I can feel that cool breeze on my face once more. When I left college I got a place with the US embassy in Paris, then Berlin and back home in Washington for many years working my way up the diplomatic ladder. And then for the past twenty years right here in London.'

'Did you ever meet JFK?'

'Yes a few times socially but he was a Senator for Massachusetts's then, not when he became President'.

'How would you describe him?'

'In a word reckless but very charming. He put you at ease at once, but I think deep down he was a wild and reckless man who would take great risks. But compared with all the other Presidents he was the best we ever had by far.'

'What about Jackie, his wife?'

'A brave lady when JFK was killed. But a vain spoilt woman, and like a lot of mega rich upper class women she had that hatred and spite towards animals, like your Royal family, she loved blood sports.'

'Yeah, but you don't like women anyway Guy.'

'That's rubbish Seb, we're not talking sex here.'

'Tell me Guy', I butted in before a cat fight started. 'Why did she marry Aristotle Onassis for Christ sake? I know the quick answer is money but I don't buy that, she was worth millions.'

'Protection Dan. She knew that the Liberal Elite planned to wipe out the Kennedy dynasty. She said when Robert was killed "I know now they plan to kill us all". The FBI and the CIA told her they could not guarantee her safety in the USA. I hope she answered "So what else is new". Onassis could protect her from her enemies. He had a private army second to none, plus private islands, planes, ocean going yachts, and fortress type mansions where she and her children would be safe. She knew they would never be safe in America. As soon as Robert said he would run for President they killed him, and her son John Kennedy Jr. stated the same thing in 1999, he too was killed.'

'You think that Guy?'

'It's common knowledge in top Government circles that his plane was sabotaged, hence it came down in the Atlantic Ocean. But you know Dan, these people we are talking about here are a different breed or species to us; our Presidents, your Kings and Queens, all powerful world leaders. Let's put it simply; they have never waited for a bus or train, never been unable to pay a bill or been out of work. All their lives they have had the best food, clothes, cars, places to live, medical treatment, education. The way a man like you lives Dan would be beyond their comprehension. There was one exception, President Ronald Reagan. He came from a very poor background, became a movie star, then Governor of California, then President.'

'Man that's going some', I said.

'You bet, and what did they do? Gunned him down in the street while our stupid Secret Service, once more, were too slow to react. He survived but never fully recovered and as a President he was finished. Tragic, because he was a good man.

We have a very bad track record for killing our Presidents; JFK, Garfield, McKinley and Lincoln were all murdered. Mind you I'm not too upset about Lincoln, he started our civil war and we lost over 600,000 good Americans. Four more Presidents were badly wounded; Jackson, both the Roosevelts and Reagan. Truman only just missed a couple of bullets. Now if you dig deep enough in almost every one of those cases the reasons were to do with massive amounts of Government money, being controlled by International Bankers.'

'Like they say Guy, money is the root of all evil, and you knew Ray and Kilgallen?

'I knew Johnnie very well.' *So I've heard* I thought to myself, then caught Seb's eye, his look warned me not to say anything before Guy continued:

'Dorothy I only met once but knew all about her because she was famous. Johnnie was known to us all at that time as JR. He was an incredible entertainer in his time, maybe the biggest star on earth six years before Elvis and without doubt the first Rock n Roller. Sinatra killed off his career early.'

'Yeah I heard about that.'

'Dorothy was a fearless journalist in the real sense of the word, hundred per cent professional. When she went down to Texas to meet Jack Ruby he must have told her something or said something that put her onto the biggest scoop of her life. She took her notes back to New York, then made contact with the White House where she knew all the top people. But more importantly she knew the two women closest to JFK; his lovers Mary Myer and Florence Smith. They were heartbroken and mad as only women can be so they told Dorothy everything that JFK had told them, and it was plenty.

Now JFK knew he was in danger because he would not agree to the horrendous plans for the New World Order so he had copies made. I am sure his brother Robert had one and would have gone public with it had he become President, that's why they killed him, and one went to Mary and Florence, and that's why they were killed.'

'What about his wife Jackie?'

'No, he knew she would be too scared to deal with it. So those ladies passed them on to Dorothy. They could only have got them from JFK.'

I interrupted; 'So indirectly Jack Ruby led Dorothy not to who killed JFK but why he was killed?'

'You've got it son.'

'And when Dorothy knew the net was closing in she sent the original to JR.'

'Right again. Out of all the people Doll knew - and man she knew some - JR was the least likely to come under suspicion. She was one brave and brilliant lady. But I must stress Dan, the one she had and sent to JR, this one I have here, is the original, I repeat the original! Copies would mean nothing. Anyone could drum up a copy or even make something up.

This one is on what is called official White House parchment embossed with the eagle and has the White House watermark. And to top it all off is signed by all the top people: the Vice President LBJ, The heads of the Army, Navy, Air Force, and a whole bunch of Senators plus J.Edgar Hoover, and this is strange and interesting; it is also signed by seven of the World's top international bankers.'

'Are they Americans?'

'Three are, the others are one British, three Swiss.'

'So JR sent it to you all those years ago, why?'

'Well maybe he didn't really know what it was all about because a lot of it is in code, but man he knew it was dynamite. Doll had told him that so he realised she was murdered because of it, and all the other people too. I had been close to him and he trusted me, also he ran with a show biz crowd. I was the only high ranking Government type person he knew and could trust and on that visit to London he would have discussed in detail with me how to tell the World just what the bastards have got in store for us.

He wanted to do right by Doll, but sadly he died before that meeting could happen. He never got over her death or the way she died. He loved her very much and she him. Now these documents, more dangerous than an atomic bomb, have come right down the line to me, an old timer with nowhere to run or hide.'

The room fell silent, each of us with our own thoughts. I knocked back my drink and put my empty glass on the small table beside me. Seb brought the room back to life saying 'I told you Dan you were getting into real heavy stuff with that book. Back off now. Tell Bob you'll do one about sex, drugs and Rock n Roll or just sex, like you and Della, or about me, just drugs.'

'Dan is not the type to back off, are you Dan? And it's now obvious that I have not been told the whole story.' As Guy spoke he looked at Seb then me with a sad, almost hurt expression.'

'Guy sit back, have a drink, even if it's only coffee.' I said.

Seb got up saying 'Sure I'll make you one Guy.'

I then told him all that had happened. First about the info Marie Moretti gave me.

'Yes I've heard of her Dan', he said quietly. Then I related my run in with killer Anita and how she murdered Barney, but for some reason that I can't explain I left out Zian and the entire Chinese connection. I sensed that this man loved his country so much he could never really trust anyone outside the USA. Also I could see it would be one chunk of info too far, because he was now looking real scared, then he explained why.

'That girl killer was at my embassy Dan, a friend who's in security told me and we wondered why. It seems someone high up at my embassy wants you dead but now she's dead you can bet the job has been passed on to others. They'd have me killed too if they know about this.' He pointed to the folder.

'We're not that easily rubbed out Guy. Can I take a look at this notorious folder?'

'Sure you can.' He reached over and handed me the large, surprisingly heavy envelope. The heavy parchment pages had gone slightly yellow with age but the printed text was still very clear. At the top was an embossed American Eagle turning aggressively to defend the stars and stripes above the words *Defender of Freedom*.

There was a handwritten note attached in copper plate writing stating it was from the head of the FBI, J Edgar Hoover. It was divided up into what appeared to be headed sections. Under the UK section I read about:

"Mass transit of UK workers to and from Europe". "Death penalty by firing squad for the following 30 crimes (trial by Secret Police to last no more than one hour. No appeals". "Medical doctors must put forward names of those to be considered for euthanasia due to long term illness, disablement, all aged over 55 must be automatically considered". "Strict travel restrictions for the masses. Not permitted to move out of their zone without permits". "Severe food and water rationing". "All movement must be by public transport. Private ownership of motor vehicles banned (except for class 1)". "City parks to be taken over for transit camps for workers". "Mass use of porta cabins for housing. Private ownership of property banned except for class 1 and 2". "People to bear a stamp on their forehead listing their class (1 to10)". "All classes of persons 3 to 10 must be micro chipped at birth".

I read aloud; 'At some future date it will be possible to link that chip with a central TV observation centre. Also the use of hot air balloons offers great potential for mass observation if mounted with powerful cameras that are able to zoom in on the people.'

'Well that's with us today', I continued. 'The police use Drones all the time.' Guy saw my expression becoming more shocked as I read, then asked;

'Do you think it could ever happen Dan?'

'Yes I do Guy, much quicker than people would ever think because the British have been trained from school days by the Liberal Elite media to accept the unthinkable with resignation and never answer back. As far as the UK is concerned it could be brought in overnight.

Take compared to this a small example, of how the public will accept anything they're told to; smoking, OK it's bad for your health. So why not ban alcohol and sex? To have a cigarette a couple of years ago was cool and social, now it's criminal. You turn on the TV news what do you get? Football or cricket! Is that really news?

Don't forget the media have been dumbing down and brainwashing our people for over 40 years. It's got to the stage now where they think the actors in the daily soaps are real people! What are these sections Guy?' I pointed out a whole chunk of pages that seemed to be in a foreign language or more like hieroglyphics.

'Yes I noticed that. It's in code Dan so it must be bad.' I thought to myself if Zian gets his hands on it the Chinese will soon decipher every word.

'Could it be any worse than what I've read so far?'

'No indeed not, no wonder JFK would have no part of it, bless him. They intended phasing it in from 1963 to 1975. You can imagine what the latest version would read like, especially now they have "mark of the beast" technology to help them.

If this old version were ever made public Dan, they would be exposed and have an impossible task implementing the latest version. That is, as you can see all around you being brought in by stealth more so in the UK than anywhere.' A sad silence fell over the tiny room.

Seb sipped his drink but for once said nothing; Guy finally looked up and in a voice breaking with emotion said. 'The Bastards! To do this to our great Western civilisation, to crush a noble people and turn them into caged animals, while they, the elite international super class have everything. They will still be riding point to point and shopping at Harrods.'

To my surprise he started to cry. Seb reached out to put a hand on his shoulder, it was sad to see this gracious American so hurt. I think deep down it only now occurred to him that he'd spent his life working for them.

'You know what we are up against Dan?'

'I'm not sure about "We" Guy but what?'

'Evil son, pure evil. Dan, by now the people above me will realise that I have this.' He held up the folder. 'All embassies are full of intrigue, spies everywhere. I'm old and too tired to run. The last thing I can do for my country and square it with my maker before I meet him, is give this to you Dan.'

'Thanks for nothing Guy.'

'No please listen to me, hear me out. You are today, I'm yesterday, you're a man of action, you think fast on your feet. You're rebellious, street wise, and don't frighten easily. And a lone wolf like you can often achieve more than an army.'

'So apart from all that, you quite like me Guy?' Seb burst into one of his long laughs, Guy gave a slight smile. 'And what the hell will I do with it?'

'I don't know Dan but you will do the right thing. If I take it back now to the embassy it will be taken from me by force and I will be silenced. I trust you instinctively; maybe you already have an idea of how you can save all those to come, from this hell on earth.' They both looked at me almost pleadingly and I felt like they could see a large Chinese flag flying behind me. Maybe I should tell Guy about Zian, then again maybe not.

I realised this highly dangerous ball was now firmly in my court. I have to admit also that I thought anything so important to so many powerful people must be worth a few quid. OK so I've got a real greed for money. Just then my mobile rang.

'Excuse me', I said as I checked the number, it was Zian. Seb started telling Guy about the play based on his life that was due to open soon.

'Is it OK to speak Mr Dan, are you alone?'

'No not really Bob, so far I've done 35,000 words', I bluffed.

'OK I will make it very quick but must tell you now, too important to call back later. My Uncle in Frisco tell me three top killers have been dispatched to London. It must be to do with JFK folder because Maria Morretti has been taken in for questioning by CIA so be very careful my friend. You get in trouble you call at once OK?'

'When will they get here?' I asked. 'They already here Mr Dan; two men one woman but sorry we have no description to give you. Do you have gun I gave you?'

'Yes I do.'

'You carry it now?'

'Yes I do.'

Seb and Guy were starting to look in my direction. 'Remember aim steady and squeeze trigger. Don't pull or yank OK. I with you in my heart Mr Dan.'

'Thanks Bob I'll get to work on that part right away.' I put the phone away saying 'That's Bob chasing me up about the book' as I got up to leave.

'Young man', said Guy as he struggled to get to his feet. 'I wish we had met long ago because you belong to another time, a time when men were more dangerous and exciting and above all more likeable.'

I laughed because I couldn't think of a reply then said, 'We'll meet again Guy, when I'll have more time to enjoy your interesting conversation, and Guy I promise I'll try and put this', I held up the folder, 'in the hands of those where it will do most good for the poor people of the West.'

'I know you will Dan, and Dan look out for our friend Seb here for me. He's such a danger to himself and he means so much to me.'

'No worries Guy, he'll be fine, anyone hurts Seb they hurt me and I don't like that.'

Chapter 12 – Sexy Barmaids And Hero Cops

I cut through the back streets stopping off in Berwick market to buy a couple of shirts from a stall that sells real class items. Then on to the corner of Beak Street and Great Poultney Street where there's a tiny pub that I call in on when I want to be quiet and think. Bridie the Irish barmaid from my local greeted me; she works in several pubs around Soho.

'Any news Danny-Boy about Barney's killers?'

'Not that I've heard Bridie.'

'What'll it be handsome?'

'Large scotch, no ice.' She lent right over the bar to hand me my drink showing her large, gorgeous tits almost coming free from her low cut blouse. She knew I couldn't take my eyes off them so I said 'Why do you do this Bridie? You know I'm a tit man so is it to make me keep buying more drinks?'

'No', she said with a wicked smile 'it's because I'm a born prick teaser. Anyway I had you down as a leg man. Invite me up to you flat one afternoon and we can go into it in more detail.'

'What would your husband Michael', (incidentally also known as *Mad Mick),* 'have to say?'

'Oh go on now, and you a cage fighter. Don't tell me you're scared of a poor old Irish nut case?'

'Having seen him chuck out drunken yobs half his age on a Saturday night, yes I'm very scared.'

She suddenly went serious and looking over my shoulder said 'I can smell them a mile away, the *Fuzz* have just come in.'

I looked in the large glass mirror behind the bar and saw the reflection of Mills, the Scots cop. 'Daniel old friend I've been looking for you.' He struck me as being too friendly for my own good.

'The name's Dan. I can't stand Daniel.'

'Know how you feel. I'm a Donald but like to be called Jock.'

'Any news about those who killed my old pal, Donald?'

'Well, yes and no. Anyway what'll you have?'

'Large scotch, no ice', Bridie gave me a wink as he ordered it and for himself a large vodka and lime. 'Should you be drinking on duty Jock?'

'Not on duty, been taken off the Barney case. I told them no way, me and my team are making good headway, but they said MI5 Special Branch are taking over. I said *what over the death of a poor old tailor guy?* No damn way. So the bastards suspended me, me! After eighteen years' service. Dan, tell me who the hell was Barney?'

'He wasn't anyone, just a nice old man troubling no one.'

'Well hear this Dan', he said lowering his voice to a whisper. 'A young woman's body was found naked in Hyde Park. No sign of sexual assault but no clothing, and nothing to go on. She'd been shot twice at close range then fallen from a great height on to a hard surface and her hand was badly damaged, three of the fingers on her left hand were a hell of a mess, broken and hanging off, looked like a savage dog bite.'

'Yeah, well much as I love them I don't have a dog, nor did Barney. She must have known some real nasty people.' His face remained grim.

'She was rather nasty herself. It turns out, according to Interpol, that she was a contract killer from Sweden.'

Bluffing like hell I said, 'Don't tell me someone put out a contract on Barney because the jacket he made them didn't fit that good.'

'Real funny Dan, see if this makes you laugh. We found a palm print on Barney's work bench and it was hers.'

'You can't be serious Jock.'

'Can't I? She was in his flat and must have rested her hand on that bench.' Like she rested it on Mickey's cage I thought to myself. He knew I was involved.

'You know Dan, if my team were to search your place I think her prints would be there too.'

'If you think that why don't you get a warrant and search?' I was stalling for time. Should I slug him and run for it? Zian would hide me at his embassy.

'I've not told MI5 any of this. Let the big time shits do their own hard work.'

'Then what's your problem Jock?'

'I have three huge problems in my life: I like a drink, a flutter on the horses and I have to keep an expensive and greedy ex-wife. Now if you'd care to help me, to say the tune of a hundred a month, your secret stays with me forever.

I think you killed that woman Dan, maybe you had no choice. I can't think why anyone would want to kill you but anyway they will still bang you up for fifteen years.'

I knocked back my whiskey in one gulp then said, 'You're talking shit, and a hundred a month is a fortune to me but peanuts to a well paid cop, so why bother?'

'True, but I don't like to be greedy and let's just say you're not the only one on my books.'

'So you're putting the bite for small amounts on a whole crowd of victims like me?' I thought I'd play along for time, tell him what he wants to hear. 'OK Jock, you've got a deal. I'm skint right now but have a fight coming up in a week', I was lying and stalling at the same time.

I waved goodbye to Bridie and as we stepped out into the sunshine a large heavy pale green old motor bike caught my eye, it was parked on its stand by the kerb. 'What are you looking at?' asked Jock.

'That bike. It's a Sunbeam, must be someone's pride and joy. What a beauty, gotta be over fifty years old. They don't make 'em anymore, no chain, shaft drive like a car, makes for a quiet running and powerful bike.'

'You know about bikes Dan?'

'Yeah', I laughed. 'Before I went over to four wheels I was a biker like them.' Among the small group of people standing around having a drink outside in the sunshine were two bikers dressed in black leather, standing a few feet away talking quietly, drinks in hand. I thought it strange that they had their black visors down on their helmets and they turned away when I looked over at them.

'No time to discuss motorbikes Dan, let's go to your place, I have some print checking to do.'

'I take it you're back on unofficial duty Jock, do you have a warrant?'

'You bet', he said with a hint of menace in his voice, 'just don't ask to see it'. We crossed Lexington Street into Silver Place, a narrow pedestrian only walkway that runs for a few hundred yards between small shops; cars can't enter it because back in Victorian times iron bollards were placed at each end to stop horse and carts driving through.

I had to get rid of this creep, he had me by the balls. I was toying with the idea of putting a bullet in his leg and making a dash for it. As for him keeping quiet about me forever, I'd trust him as far as I'd trust Bridie the barmaid, at least being double crossed by her would be a hell of a lot more fun.

Being deep in panic-stricken thought I paid no attention to someone shouting way back behind me. Just then Jock turned round. 'Look at these stupid sods! Can't they read the *No Vehicles* sign?' It was the two bikers on the big Sunbeam coming towards us, an old woman was shouting at them because they'd knocked her shopping bag out of her hand, sending oranges and potatoes rolling across the ground like some veggie bowling alley. Jock stepped out in the middle of the walkway holding up his warrant card with one hand and waving them to stop with the other.

Then, turning to me he yelled; 'For fuck's sake Dan, he's got a shooter!' The pillion rider was holding high in the air a sawn off shotgun. Lowering it quickly over his driver's shoulder he fired but at the same time the bike's front wheel ran over one of the rolling spuds, causing the front wheel to wobble slightly. The shot went wide, slamming into the wall beside us. To my amazement Jock stepped right out blocking their path, the bike was only fifty feet away now and bearing down on us fast.

'I'm a police officer, I am ordering you to stop', he shouted. By now I had my gun in hand and took careful aim at the gunman. I knew it was me they wanted to kill. In my head I could hear Zian's clear voice; *Take aim, steady, squeeze don't pull the trigger and fire"* We both fired at the same time. Jock leapt back protectively placing himself in front of me. He took the full blast, throwing him back into the doorway. My shot hit dead on straight into the gunman's black visor, bright red blood and black plastic burst into the air. His arms flew up, the shotgun fired again as he fell back off the bike.

I swung round, following the bike as it flew past and was now turning by the bollards at the far end of the walkway, the rider had his leg on the floor speedway rider style. With engine roaring he was trying to manoeuvre the heavy bike round in a tight circle. Maybe he was coming back for his pal or to run me down, either way I admired his nerve. I would have kept going.

Jock called out in a weak voice; 'Dan, Dan, watch it he's armed.' The scumbag had reached down by the petrol tank and pulled out a long barrelled hand gun. I dropped down on one knee and took careful aim. I got off four shots; one hit the bike, the rest hit the rider. He fired once, hitting the window of the small shop we were standing next to, shattering glass in all directions. He slumped over the handlebars, the big bike slid over on its crash bar sliding and grinding along the walkway in a shower of sparks. A strange silence fell on the scene. The two bikers lay dead, the bike's engine had cut out when it went over.

A young couple and the old woman who shouted were now crouching petrified in a doorway. People and cars had stopped in Beak Street, alerted by the sound of gunfire, to watch from a safe distance what was happening, too scared to come any closer. I plugged triple nine into my mobile. 'Emergency, what service please?'

'A police officer has been shot. Send an ambulance. We're in Silver Place, Soho at the end of Beak Street, opposite end from Regents Street.' I could smell petrol real strong, maybe I hit the tank. I put my arms under Jock and dragged him fifty yards down the walk, away from danger. A thick trickle of blood was coming from the side of his mouth and nose. His voice was a whisper. He spoke slowly like he was in great pain; it was like watching a re-run of Barney's death.

'Those shits got the shock of their lives when you pulled that gun Dan.'

'You saved me Jock.'

'I was only protecting my investment, hundred a month ain't to be sniffed at.'

'I'm putting it up to two hundred', I said trying to keep him awake.

'Dan, my card.' His warrant card was laying a few feet away. I gave it to him, he clutched it to his blood soaked chest. 'Dan, being a cop was my life. I loved being in the force. I've only been bent this last year when I got in deep shit with money. I'm so ashamed Dan.'

'Jock you're a great cop, a hero. You can't wipe out eighteen years great service because of one mistake.'

'Do yer think so Dan?'

'I know so.' He gave a weak laugh, and said 'I'm dying for a fag mate.' I lit one for him and one for myself and put it gently between his lips, avoiding the trickling blood. Just then with a wailing siren an emergency ambulance pulled in at the far end of the walk, a man and girl paramedic team came running fast with their equipment.

'What can you tell us barked the girl?'

'He's a police officer, Donald Mills, but will only answer to the name Jock, and he's been hit by a shotgun blast while trying to protect the public. The man's a hero.'

The male medic then spotted the two bikers. 'Who the hell are they?'

'They're the ones who shot him, and they're dead.'

'And you sir?'

'I'm a police officer too, now cut the questions or I'll report you both. Get to work fast on this police officer right now!' I shouted. They began loosening his tie and throwing his fag to one side they placed an oxygen mask on his face. I ran over to the Sunbeam heaving it upright, it weighed a ton. I tightened the petrol cap. It had been leaking out forming a pool between the two bikers. I swung my leg over and kicked down the starter, she fired like a vintage Rolls, the medics had Jock on one of those trolley stretchers with wheels and were running him into the ambulance. I pulled alongside, reached over and ruffled his hair. He opened his eyes and winked, then closed them again slowly saying; 'At least I'm dying a hero Dan.'

I put the bike on it's stand, went back, picked up Jock's fag and flicked it over onto the bikers. With a loud whoosh the alley was engulfed in a sheet of red and orange flame. *What's it all coming to?* I thought. *Open air cremations on the Soho Streets!* I ran back to the bike and was away. That will give MI5 a few problems, trying to get DNA from those two murdering bastards.

Chapter 13 – To Be Alone And Afraid Is A Crushing Thing

As I cut out into Oxford Street three squad cars sped past me answering my 999 call. Riding the Sunbeam was like driving a WW2 tank with turbo. At the top of the Kingsway I pulled over and called Della.

'I need help like never before Del, where are you?'

'I'm driving sweetheart, down the Old Kent Road. I've been doing some nude pin up stuff in town.'

'Please Del, turn around, meet me half way. I'm heading towards you.' There was a long pause.

'OK, this better be serious stuff.'

'It is Del, believe me, it is. Where shall we meet?'

'You're the problem Dan, you tell me.'

'OK, about half way, the Cut.'

'Where the hell is that?'

'It runs by the side of the "Old Vic" theatre.'

'Yeah OK I know it. I'll be there in twenty minutes.'

'Bless you Della.' I pulled away flat out, jumping red lights round the Aldwych and along the Strand. But as I went to turn left over Waterloo Bridge a black cab pulled across me blocking me in.

The cabbie yelled; 'Where's your crash helmet? Don't you know it's illegal to ride without one?'

'I don't have to I'm a Sikh.'

'OK so where's your turban?' I jumped off the bike lent in the cab and stuck my gun right in his face.

'OK arsehole, pull back and let me through, or I'll blow your face in half.' I thought the cab was backfiring but it was the sound of him farting. He went deathly white and reversed the cab fast! As I got back on the bike I put a bullet in his front nearside tyre, it went down with a loud hiss, then another in the radiator.

The driver of the bus that was blocked in behind me pulled back his side window and called out 'That's the best road rage I've seen this week!'. I tore over the bridge. Then passing Waterloo station on my right the old bike began to splutter; she'd run out of petrol. I rolled round left into the cut and coasted into a small street at the back of the "Old Vic".

I floored the bike then ran round to the front of the "Old Vic". As I did so Della, with tyres squealing, was making a U-Turn outside the theatre in the "Hat". I leapt in and she pulled away fast.

'Did I see you riding a big motorbike?'

'Yes you did.'

'Man that's a first!' She threw her head back laughing, showing that perfect set of gleaming white teeth, making me know how much I'd missed her.

'I'll explain all later but for now where can you hide me?'

'You'll be safe with me down in Brixton even the law don't move in there without my friend Win's say so.'

'Who's that?'

'Winston De Silver and his crew. They run everything, he's the man!'

'Can we have the top up Della, I don't want to be seen?'

'Sure we can, man you must really be in big bother.' With that the metal hard top folded out of the boot and dropped into place over our heads. I took out my gun and began to re-load it.

'I'll say one thing for you Dan', she said looking at the gun. 'You're never boring; off beat, crazy, even stupid, and at times like now, fucking dangerous but never boring, and man I hate boring people.'

'Are we there yet Della?'.

She laughed.

'We will be in less than thirty minutes. Further down I'll do a right, we'll cut through Peckham and on into Brixton. It's the Caribbean without the sunshine. I've told Winston about you so you're OK, but don't say any more than you have to, cos a lot of these guys are Yardies, you follow me?'

'Sure I don't know nothing and never saw you before in my life.'

'Is that the JFK book tucked inside your coat?'

'I've got the book on a memory stick, but yes this is sure connected with it.'

'Well if it's causing this sort of real heavy agro like you having to carry a gun why the hell do you bother?'

'You know me Della I don't like to back down.' I wondered if she would believe me if I told her that so far I'd had to kill three people before they killed me, and at least one other had been killed? All because of the incredible contents of this large envelope. Come to think about it, I can't believe it myself.

We were now crawling along at 5mph in real heavy traffic because of massive road works. My mobile rang so I told Della to put up the windows to cut out the sound of the road workers drilling.

'Is that you Dan?'

'Hi Seb.'

'Are you driving Dan?'

'No I'm in the car, but Della's driving. What's wrong Seb? You sound awful?'

'Bad, bad news Dan', he started to cry. I had the mobile on speaker phone so I could hear above the roadworks but that meant Della could also hear him.

She leant over and said in a stage whisper 'He's stoned out of his head. Tell him to lay off that fucking crack.'

'I heard that bitch. I'm not on anything except a small whisky, but I will be later. I'm gonna go wild, I won't come down for days. I've got to block out the pain. Remember I love you both, please come and be with me, please Dan. You know Dan to be alone and afraid is a crushing thing.'

'OK Seb take it easy now, tell me what's wrong pal?'

'Guy's dead!' he screamed. There was a long pause while my stunned brain took in the shock.

'What the hell happened Seb?' Between sobs he continued. 'When he left here just after you, he got a cab back to his embassy in Grosvenor Square. The cab stopped at the lights in Bond Street, two men pulled up next to him on a motorbike. The pillion rider jumps off, reaches in through the window and stabs Guy in the arm with a hypo needle. The bastard calmly gets back on the bike and they speed off. Guy collapses and is dead in seconds. The cabbie tried to save him, the ambulance got there very quick but no use.

The police have been here for ages, Guy had my address in his wallet, asking all sorts of weird questions. They were plain clothes. I didn't like the way they spoke to me so I told them nothing. I didn't mention about you being here or about that folder that Guy gave you.'

'Thanks Seb, well done.'

I thought to myself, they were MI5 and they must have known that he'd just left Seb's place.

'Dan, was this anything to do with that NWO business you were both talking about and the documents he gave you?'

'Yes it was. Now Seb, listen to me like never before, I swear that what I'm going to tell you is the truth OK?'

'Yeah Dan I'm listening. The two who killed Guy came straight on to get me. They caught up with me in Silver Place. I looked at my watch. About an hour ago I killed them about two seconds before they killed me, you'll hear all about it on tonight's TV news.'

'Well done Dan, that makes me feel better, I'll rest easier knowing that.'

'I've got to lay low for a while Seb, Della is going to hide me with people she knows down in Brixton.'

'Be careful Dan, you could run into all kinds of trouble down there.'

'Get away from your place for a few days Seb. I'll keep in touch and we'll go together to Guy's funeral.'

'Thanks for that Dan, I couldn't face it alone. You know Guy liked you. One of the last things he said was "Dan's OK, he'll do what's right with that folder".'

'I'll try my best, now Seb I know you're hurting so promise you'll take care.'

'I'll be OK. I might go round to Mike Shaw's studio. He wants to do a portrait of me, and he's got some great one's of James Dean that I want to buy.'

'Good idea, get out of the flat for a while. Or get a cab down here and hang out with me and Della.'

'Dan, you know I never leave Soho, but if those shits come back bullying me again I will.'

'Is that a promise Seb?'

'Yeah it is. See you soon Dan, take care, love to Della.'

Now free of the roadworks the little Hat was starting to pick up speed.

'Who was Guy?' Della asked lowering the windows once more. 'And why did two bikers take him out for Christ sake?'

'He was an old American diplomat; a real gentleman. Met him once and liked him.'

'You? Mixing with gentlemen and diplomats? You're really moving up in the world Dan, and I had you down as a broken down cage fighter and my bit of rough.'

The words *broken down* hurt. So that's how she sees me, but I said nothing. She pressed a number on the speaker phone.

'Is Winston handy?'

'No Della he's out on business. This is Delroy can I help?'

'Yeah I need backup to bring me in. I've got a tail, could be the Fuzz or that North London crew Winston's at war with.'

'OK Del where you at?'

'In fifteen minutes I'll be crossing Peckham Rye Park.'

'You driving that little silver sports?'

'That's me Delroy.'

'We're on our way in the Hummer and fully tooled up.'

'What the hell was that all about Della?'

'Since we left the "Old Vic" there's been a learner car keeping up with us.'

'You mean a learner driver?'

She nodded then looking in the rear view mirror said, 'And it's still there hanging in real close.' I turned round and saw right behind us a bright red mini with a driving school sign on the roof.

'I know they use Minis Della but not like that. That one's a top of the range "Mini Cooper D". No driving school would use that, they cost over twenty grand! Why didn't you tell me before?'

'Cos you were talking to Seb about shoot-outs in Soho and busy loading guns and stuff.'

'Can you see who's driving?'

'No, blacked out windows.' The car phone rang.

'Who's the enemy Della? Give us a run down.'

'My friend tells me it's a red "Mini Cooper D" with a driving school sign on the roof, over and out. Is this maybe your problem Dan?'

'Could well be Della.'

Yeah, I thought to myself, there are still killers out there waiting for me, and oh Christ, I forgot that trace Zian fixed to my car; it must still be sending out a signal. You can bet they have hacked into it, that's how they picked us up.'

Della could sure handle this little tornado, moving up and down through the gears like a jack in the box. The tiny engine was screaming as we overtook trucks and buses, weaving in and out of the traffic. We were now doing over 70 in a 30 mph zone, but the Mini stuck to us like glue. Then Della's phone rang again, she pressed the button. A woman's voice with super posh English accent said;

'McQuade, toss the folder out the window, I'll stop and collect it, end of story. Refuse and you're both dead and I still get the folder. Have a nice day.'

I started to pull out the folder from inside my jacket. Della put her hand over mine to stop me and yelled into the speaker; 'Bollocks you slag!'

Scared but laughing I said, 'Della that's what I love about you, such class, so ladylike.' With that she swung out to overtake a line of traffic. As she pulled in again she flashed her lights at an oncoming massive black 4X4 6L V8 Hummer H2 with gigantic crash bars. Then a loud crack as a bullet came through the back window and hit the windscreen making a neat hole between us. The Hummer made a screaming handbrake turn and pulled in close behind the mini. Another shot hit the dashboard smashing the phone and turning the screen into a spider's web pattern.

Della was now driving blind so I kicked out the glass. Looking behind I saw the mini pulling out over the white line. The driver's arm was out of the window, gun in hand, taking aim and it was good as she blew out both our rear tyres. We hit the kerb, slammed over the pavement and were now sliding over the grass and into a low wall with an expensive smash.

Della said; 'I would have thought that mixing with the sort of people you do you would have invested in run-flat tyres'.

Back on the road the Hummer was now ramming the Mini at full speed. It came off the road and rolled a couple of times and then slammed into a huge oak tree that must have been there at least 200 years. I heard screaming from inside the Mini, then watched in horror as the Hummer reversed for about 50 yards, then accelerated forward and slammed into the little car crushing it with it's heavy front crash bars, the screaming stopped.

Next it reversed at speed across the grass to us. By now we had scrambled out of my beloved *Hat,* now reduced to a roofless wreck, shaken but not badly hurt, thanks to the *Hat's* roll bar.

A gruff voice shouted, 'Come on, let's be gone outta here. Brixton's calling me!' We scrambled up into the Hummer, but not before I unclipped the tracer from under the front wing of the hat. As we passed the crushed Mini I saw a woman's arm with heavy bracelets hanging limply out of the window.

'She's got to be dead Della', I said.

'Ain't that a shame, Dan?' she laughed.

'And if it wasn't for the boys here it would have been us.'

'That must have been the third assassin Zian warned me about or, with that accent, maybe MI5.'

'Who cares, whoever she was, she ain't anymore' said Della with one of her put-down stares.

Chapter 14 – The 'Hat' Goes On Ebay

We pulled up at a huge Victorian house festooned with CCTV cameras and iron grills at all the windows, plus some expensive motors in the driveway. I noticed an Alfa and a Porsche, plus two real heavy minders on the door.

Della's flat within the house was neat and expensively furnished.

'OK to use the computer Dell?'

'Sure, feel free' she called out from the kitchen.

I switched on and inserted my JFK memory stick. The word count told me so far I'd done over 50,000 words. I put my small voice recorder on the desk and let it run and at the same time began to type like a man possessed. A couple of hours later Della came in with two coffees. She almost had on a sexy little nightdress plus high heels, and was fully made up. It didn't take much working out that this was akin to wearing full war paint and being dressed for combat, bearing in mind that it was only 7pm! Sipping her coffee suggestively, and then nodding to her large bed, she said;

'Fancy a romp?' The short answer to that was a definite yes! Both she knew and I knew, I could never resist her. In no time her powerful legs were wrapped around me, sending me into the land of ecstasy. During the next couple of hours I made love to her in every position imaginable, some known only to those who live in Soho. I could never get enough of her. Eventually she left me lying on the bed exhausted, while she took a shower singing at the top of her voice. I took that as a sign that I'd pleased her. She came back into the room and sat naked at her dressing table pulling faces as she put on fresh lipstick. I came up behind her putting my hands around her large firm breasts.

'No Dan darling, you've had enough for one day. Take a shower and do some more to your book.'

'OK I know when I've been dismissed'. I took a shower and on returning to the room the cold air struck me. She had opened all the windows.

'Shit Dell do'yer want me to get pneumonia?'

'I'm getting rid of the evidence, letting the steam from the shower out now get dressed and quick', she said throwing me my shirt. 'If Winston catches us like this he'll cut your balls off with that machete he carries.'

'None of his fucking business! or is it Della?'

'You may as well know Dan, me and him are an item.' She said it matter of factly.

'Oh yeah where does that leave me?'

'Like I told you, you're my bit of rough. When I'm shopping in the West End I'll call and see you. Dan, I want to be married and I'd like three kids before I'm thirty.'

'I don't see much call Della for a pregnant stripper with a big band aid on her arse.'

'Real funny Dan, a girl's gotta be practical. Winston can buy a house with cash for me out Bromley way. What can you offer, a run down one bedroom rented flat. No contest!' She laughed and squeezed my balls gently saying, 'That's the deal Dan, take it or leave it.' With that she danced out of the room.

All in all Della, I thought to myself, I think I'll leave it. Zian once said "Work is the ultimate salvation". So I turned on the computer again and started to type like crazy. I finally fell asleep over the keyboard at 5am. I woke around 9am, washed then borrowed an electric shaver from one of Winston's men and made myself look half decent. Then without a knock, the door opened and in came a smartly dressed West Indian guy. As he gave me a high five I noticed he wore a large flashy ring on almost every finger.

'Winston', he announced. 'We meet at last Dan. I've watched your fights on TV and read your articles in "Fighter" magazine. Man you took a bad beating in that last fight.' He had a London accent and a voice any actor would die for.

'Thanks for hiding me out Winston, I'm very grateful.'

'No problem. You're untouchable here on my territory; no one ventures into this area without me knowing or without my permission, including the law. Della

159

tells me you're friends from way back, so you're OK by me.' I thought it best to let that statement pass without comment. 'I had your Daihatsu sports collected and put in one of my workshops. It's a write off but we'll get the insurance money for you.'

'Big problem Winston, the car wasn't insured; I couldn't afford it.' He seemed to find that very funny. When he stopped laughing he said, 'Tell you what, my guys will break it up for spares. They will fetch around a grand on eBay, so I'll give you half, five hundred right now, and I'll have 500 later. Have we got a deal?'

'Sure have. Thanks for helping me out.' Sadly I thought to myself just a few hours ago my lovely little car was worth around four grand! With that he took a wad of fifties out of his inside pocket, counted out ten and handed them to me.

'You can put all the paperwork in the post to me later OK. You've left quite a trail behind you on your way to Brixton. Why are so many people trying to kill you?'

I thought, be careful. If I've got this guys mark right and I think I have, he's a charming, ruthless nutter.

'I'm writing a book about President Kennedy and they think I know who pulled the trigger and want to stop me telling the world that it was the Mafia.' My stupid answer seemed to stop his questions for now, but once he realised that people who would kill for something would also pay massive money for the same thing, it would dawn on him real quick that there was much more to it than I was saying. And if he smelt mega bucks he'd become extremely dangerous.

'You lay low Dan. Get on with your book, no problem, OK? Hey I gotta question. Saw you on that late *Sport Today* show being interviewed about you going over to cage fighting. You looked real smart wearing a light blue sports jacket, who's your tailor?'

'He was a lovely old guy with a small workshop below my flat but he died suddenly a few days ago.'

'Man that's sad. I get all my gear in Mayfair, I might try that new guy in Savile Row where all the boy bands and Simon Cowell get their clothes.'

'No rubbish, Winston, if I were Simon Cowell's tailor I'd prefer to remain anonymous. All I ever see him dressed in is a scruffy black T-Shirt!'

He threw his head back and laughed long and loud then said, 'Man I've got work to do. I'll see yer.'

Chapter 15 – The Terrible Death Of JFK, Seen On Screen

I pressed on with the book. The words just flowed, I was on a writing roll. I worked flat out until gone midnight, did a word count, well over 65,000, then a spell check that took another hour of corrections. I saved it all and shut down. For the first time in ages I felt dead tired but relaxed. All the running, killing and madness of the last couple of days was losing its edge. I lay back on the bed and lit a fag.

A faint tap on my door broke the stillness. Della came quietly into the room, she looked grim.

'Don't you think we're pushing our luck?' I asked.

'I'm not here for that Dan. I've got bad news, real bad.'

'OK let's have it.'

She gave a long sigh and dropped the evening paper beside me on the bed, then said quietly, 'Seb's dead.' The headline she pointed to read "Sebastian Horsley found dead at his home today".

'Oh Christ, no don't tell me this Dell.' Tears filled my eyes and I couldn't read any further. 'How did it happen?' I asked.

'According to the paper a heroin and cocaine overdose. He was a lovely, sweet crazy guy,' she replied softly.

'Bob was going to put his artwork on the website, those shark paintings would have made him world famous. He would have loved it, you know he was a writer, poet, painter.'

She smiled sadly and said, 'If he were here now he'd say; *and don't forget sex maniac!* He didn't belong in this age Dan, he was too flamboyant, too human.'

'If I caused his death I couldn't live with it Dell.'

'You mean this NWO thing?'

'Yeah, they killed his pal Guy.'

'There's no mention of foul play and face it Dan, he was an addict.'

'I know but somehow I don't buy it. I'll tell you one thing for sure; without him Soho will never be the same. You know I feel like how those Victorian friends of Oscar Wilde must have felt when they heard of his death.'

'How old was he Dan?'

'Around forty-seven, but looked younger.'

'Try and get some rest, I'll see you in the morning,' Della said as she kissed me on the cheek and left the room. I just sat there stunned and sad for ages. Then my mobile rang. Get some rest! Fat chance I thought.

'Dan, how's it going?' It was Bob.

'If I tried to answer that we'd be on the phone till next week. The book is well over three quarters finished and is running at just under 70,000 words.'

'Good man. I'm in New York about to get on the plane home. Get it to my office soon as poss, my two proof readers and the typesetter are ready and waiting. They'll get started on it right away. I'll be there in around ten hours from now, bye.'

The next morning Della got one of Winston's motorcycle messengers to take my memory stick up town to the Stagedoor office. I handed over the stick, shaped like a lipstick just to be extra careful, with some notes and off it went. Then I put a call in to Zian.

'Don't ask me how but I've got the documents you want.' There was a long pause.

'I did suspect that Mr Dan. I have been seeing amazing news items on TV about shootings and murders. Also a police officer being killed trying to protect a young man in the West End. That made me put two and two together and decided that my old friend was very much involved. I see your car is in Railton Road Brixton. Why are you there?'

'My car, Zian, is no more and is in many pieces miles away. Your tracer is on the desk beside me.'

'You resourceful man Mr Dan. You have done well.' We both knew it was a sure bet that other people were listening in on our rather guarded conversation.

'We meet soon Mr Dan.' Our eavesdroppers now knew where I was and that Zian was on his way to me, and that these priceless world changing documents were about to change hands.

As I put the phone down I realised how relieved I was to know that I'd soon be handing them over, then I remembered I'd forgotten the DVD Bob gave me. I tipped out my travel bag and there it was. The label said "This is the world famous home movie shot by a bystander with a standard 8 movie camera on Friday November 22 1963 at 12.30pm midday". I slipped it in the DVD drive and clicked on full screen turned on the speakers, poured a sherry from Della's drinks cabinet and sat back in her big armchair.

There was the President and his wife Jackie arriving at the airport; a real good looking couple, more like movie stars than politicians. The crowds are going wild, shaking hands and chatting to well-wishers all around them. Then they are in the car sitting in the back of the big open top shiny Lincoln; Governor John Connally of Texas and his wife Nellie in front, and in front of them Roy Kellerman, bodyguard, Secret Service and the driver an Irishman William Greer, also Secret Service.

The sun's out, it's a great day, they look happy. There are motorcycle outrider cops around the car. Then suddenly JFK jolts back in his seat, putting his hand up to his throat, he starts sliding towards his shocked wife. Now Connally gets hit. Kellerman looks round, see's the two men are hit, but does nothing! No attempt to climb over the seats to protect JFK, nothing! Greer, the driver, slows the car to almost a stop, the brake lights go on, and he turns to look but does nothing! The few seconds that the car is moving dead slow gives the sharpshooter a perfect target; JFK's head explodes in a spray of blood.

I heard myself shout 'No, no you bastards, no one deserves that.' The motorcycle cops dropped their bikes, drew their guns and ran up the grass bank followed by several bystanders towards the sound of gunfire. Remember these cops are used to the sound of gunfire and can therefore react quickly to what direction it's coming from.

Most of the crowd have flung themselves flat on the grass to avoid more bullets flying over their heads. Jackie Kennedy panics and tries to climb out of the car. Bodyguard Clint Hill sprints from the following car, jumps up on the Lincoln and throws himself over JFK in a too late effort to protect him. The car then takes off fast to the Parkland hospital. Out of all those there to protect JFK that day, no one does anything; the response from the Secret Service was totally useless. The Dallas police did more.

Just then Della and Winston came into the room. 'Look at this!' I re-run the film. 'You actually see the poor guy get killed.'

'Hey he's lovely, a real dish, who is he?'

'He was the President of the USA.'

'The bird looks good to', said Winston.

'That's his wife.' Then came the shot of JFK being hit.

'Oh shit a lovely guy like that', yelled Della. 'Why the fuck did they do that Dan?'

'Because he wanted to change the money system in America and the banks didn't like it. Also, he wouldn't agree to their plans for a new type of world called a New World Order.'

'Look at those stupid bastards!' Winston yelled, 'Bodyguards? My boys could have protected him better. If we'd been there he'd still be alive. When was this Dan?'

'Nearly fifty years ago Win.

'Well maybe not then', he laughed. Then it came up on the screen. "Jackie never forgave the Secret Service for their non-service that day. She called their protection appalling. Driver Greer offered his total apology to Jackie. She refused it".

Then followed JFK making a speech when he says "Ask not what your country can do for you; ask what you can do for your country" and another speech where he states there are secret societies trying to take over the USA and as President he will not let that happen.

I sat stunned. Until now he was someone on the written page or someone being recalled from another person's memory. But now, to me, he has come alive. To see him moving and speaking on screen gave my whole project a massive new dimension.

Della handed round some drinks and said, 'The guy had great charisma. I wish he were around today, what a guy, I'd vote for him.'

'Me too', said Winston, 'Was anyone ever convicted for his murder?'

'No, and legal experts have proved that if Oswald had lived and been put on trial he would have been found not guilty.'

'Didn't I read somewhere, Dan, that all the info on his murder was locked away in the vaults of the White House by the US government until long after those concerned would all be dead?'

'That's right, Win. Some info was released but vital pages were missing and parts so heavily blacked out they were unreadable. All the final info is due for release in 2017. That's 55 years after JFK's murder, the crafty no good bastards! And you can bet your last pound that when

2017 arrives some shit will slap another 20 years on the release date.'

Just then one of Win's men stuck his head round the door saying, 'Boss there's a Chinese guy to see Dan.'

'Sure, show him up.' Zian glided into the room, his movements reminded me of a Panther when moving slowly through the grass. I introduced everyone.

Della in her abrupt way said, 'I hear you have a very attractive girlfriend, where is she?'

'Ah, Jia-Li. No she not girlfriend that is only act we put on for our under cover work at the Embassy.' *You could have fooled me*, I thought to myself.

'She married in China to high ranking official in government. Right now she cover for me at Embassy. We use double, a man who look like me leave Embassy with Jia-Li get underground train to north London. I slip away via concealed door at back of building, fast car bring me here. I lay on back seat all the way. It is very dangerous to be a decoy but she very professional and tough lady but I worry that she be OK.'

'So what now Zian?' I asked with some trepidation.

'I go to South Coast, meet with fast motor boat who take me middle of English Channel. There one of our navy ships disguised as Chinese freighter will slow just long enough to winch me aboard. She carry no cargo so very fast and is heavily armed. Later on French coast near

Biarritz I transfer to plane to Beijing so within 48 hours entire plans for New World Order will be in hands of Chinese government.

Winston smiled and said, 'You sound like 007 Zian.'

'No, Mr Winston, James Bond entertainment, but this is deadly serious.'

I then took him into Della's room. 'Here it is Zian.' I handed him the thick folder, he looked stunned.

'You are remarkable man Mr Dan.'

'Not really, I had some lucky breaks.' Then I related the whole story how, through Seb, I met Guy and unknown to him the folder was stored for years in the back of the painting, where Johnnie Ray had hidden it after Dorothy Kilgallen sent it to him, just before she was murdered. How the two killer bikers got blown away thanks to a hero policeman who got killed protecting me; the woman Mini driving assassin who got crushed to death by Winston's private army for trying to kill me and Della. And how tragically Seb and Guy were also now dead. For once the usually cool confident Zian looked tired and worried, not to mention scared by all that I had told him.

'Please Mr Dan, can I be left alone to read through these incredible documents?'

'Sure, I'll be with Del and Win.'

After the best part of an hour Zian reappeared looking dazed and shocked then said, 'There is no doubt these are the original, genuine documents. And the contents are even worse than I ever could have imagined and I would say that a third of it has already come to pass and is in place; like CCTV and a mass database of information storage; and the increasing use of satellites; and drones for spying on the public.'

Then looking around he asked, 'Do you have a way that I can make a copy of this?'

'Sure', said Della taking him through to the computer, scanner and printer. I didn't bother to ask but wondered why he wanted a copy.

While the scanner was running he came back and said; 'The last part of my journey will be the most dangerous. Could you escort me, Mr Winston? My government will pay you well of course.'

'Zian, when you talk money you're talking my language. We'll take one of the Hummers and six of my best men; one driver, five minders. We will be armed with Stens.'

I must have looked puzzled because he left the room and came back two minutes later carrying a couple of strange looking guns with open metal stock and short barrels.

'I recently did a deal with some people in Dublin. Way back in the 70's the IRA got into an army ordinance depot in Bicester near Oxford, got away with these Sten guns, plus 303s, Revolvers, Grenades and Bren Guns. It cost me fifty grand, but I've got enough firepower to tool up an army. When trouble starts on the streets I'll sell to the highest bidder and my investment will multiply by ten or even twenty!'

Chapter 16 – The Year Of The Dragon

As we got into the Hummer Zian turned towards me saying; 'Mr Dan, you take the folder for last part of journey.'

'What the hell for Zian? I'm glad to see the back of what is probably the most dangerous reading matter on earth.'

'Well you know we Chinese are very superstitious. If anything happen to me it very safe with my young fighter friend.'

'OK, but you're being a pain in the arse.' I tucked the large folder inside my coat for the last time. The journey to the Sussex coast was uneventful except when we came up fast behind a slow moving huge supermarket truck pulling a long trailer, the truck being so wide we couldn't get past. Our driver flashed his headlights but got no response.

One of the men said, 'See that roundabout up ahead? Once passed that it's only a country lane so you'll never get past if you don't now.' With that Win grabbed one of the Sten guns, opened the sun roof, stood up on the seat and fired a burst at the trailer's two double wheels; it sank almost onto its axels, large chunks of black rubber tyre flew up hitting the Hummer. The truck driver's dash must have lit up like a Christmas tree. On went the hazard and brake lights and he slowed and pulled onto the grass verge.

As we sped past, Win still head and shoulders out of the roof yelled at the truck, 'Show some respect man!'. With that he fired a couple more bursts into the air. I thought to myself not only were you and Della made for each other, you deserve each other.

Zian directed us to a deserted track half covered in shingle; no sign of anything or anybody for miles. It was dark and silent except for the tide being in and the sound of waves breaking on the beach just a few yards away.

'Where the hell are we Zian?' I asked. 'We're in Sussex on the Pevensey marshes, they stretch for miles my friend.' We all clambered out of the Hummer. Like trained soldiers the men spaced out taking up positions around us. Zian handed a cheque to Win and asked, 'Will this be suitable Mr Winston?'

'Ten grand, that's fine by me pal as long as this baby don't bounce. I see it's payable by the Bank of China, that ain't the same as the bank of Toyland is it? Cos if it does I'll be coming out to China to find you.'

I didn't like him saying that so butted in, 'This is one stand up guy Win, you have my word, so don't talk to him that way.'

'OK, OK, take it easy Dan. Now what sort of trouble are you expecting Zian?'

'None I hope, if Jia-Li has led them away from us in London. The launch will be here in few minutes, we small bit early.'

Me and Zian walked over the wet, sliding shingle to the water's edge. He turned, gripped my arm saying; 'Come with me Mr Dan, you love Shanghai. It is what New York and London were 25 years ago. Shanghai Alpha city a World city. We go into business together make many money, lovely girls there, they like you very much.'

'I'm sure I'd like them too, but I'm a Londoner, can't leave the old place.'

He looked disappointed then said "A savage loves his native shore"

'Confucius?' I asked.

'No Mr Dan, Irish poet, James Orr, 1770 to 1816.'

'The sooner you get on that boat Zian the better, you're doing my head in!'

'How old are you Mr Dan?'

'23 but the last week working on this JFK book has aged me 40 years so I feel a clapped out 63!'

'So you born 1988 the year of the Dragon, the Dragon enjoys a very high reputation in Chinese culture. Dragon people are healthy, move quickly, can be excitable, they are honest, sensitive, and brave. Other people have confidence in them and trust them. But you have a weakness. Dragon people tend to be soft hearted and your enemies will take advantage of that.'

'OK I'll try and toughen up my heart. I think I can hear the sound of diesel engines out there, must be your motor launch.'

Just then Winston yelled out, 'Zian, Dan, a car is creeping along the track towards us with no lights.' We both drew our guns.

Winston called again, 'Say the word Zian and we'll cut the bastards down.' With that Winston's men turned on the powerful spot light mounted on the Hummer's roof. It lit up the beach and what looked like a Dodge Ram. Three men and a woman were getting out and heading our way.

'You've gone as far as you're going lady. Stop now or get you're head blown in two, I shouted.'

'You misjudge situation Mr Dan', Zian whispered, 'Jia-Li is out of range.'

'Christ you're right, it's Jia-Li.' We both lowered our guns. She wore a long stylish coat and colourful headscarf, then I saw the long barrelled hand gun. She pointed it at Zian. There were three Chinese guys carrying shotguns who stayed about 25 yards behind her, and a couple more who stayed by the car.

'Those shotguns Mr Dan are Browning Auto 5 semi-automatic mag capacity 3.3 shot shells calibre, 12 gauge…'

'Yeah, yeah, I know what you're trying to tell me Zian you long-winded Chinaman. When they start shooting we're fucking dead.'

'Please Mr Dan, don't let your last words in this World be swear words, you soon face your ancestors.'

'Yeah, when I do I'll kick some arse for getting my head blown off at 23 for Christ's sake!'

In a soft but demanding voice Jia-Li said, 'Drop your gun Zian and give me the folder.' I cursed myself for having put my gun back in its holster inside my coat. To my surprise he threw his gun onto the pebbles in front of him, then called out to Winston.

'What is effective range of your old Sten guns?'

Win called back, 'They will kill up to 35 yards, wound maybe up to 50; each clip holds 32 rounds, can fire bursts or single shots. OK, so at around a 100 she is way out of range but my boys and me will come running and firing at the same time and the spot light is in their eyes. We have our backs to it.'

Jia-Li spoke again, 'Your men would have to cover 50 yards before we come into range. By that time I will have killed both of you. Also we have other weapons.' She called out some command in Chinese over her shoulder to the men by her car. There was a loud bang then a whining whooshing sound and a small derelict beach hut further

179

along the beach exploded in a bright red fireball lighting up the dark night.

Winston called out, 'No contest Zian. They've got a grenade launcher. They can take out the Hummer and my boys in two hits, but us Brixton boys don't take no shit. Say the word and we still come running. It's your call Zian.'

He looked around for a few very long seconds then said, "A good General knows when to retreat".

'This ain't no time for Confucius Zian', I shouted.

'Not Confucius my friend, Napoleon, leader of France 1769 to 1821.' Turning to Jia-Li he said, 'I do not have Folder Mr Dan has it. He was just about to hand it to me when you arrived. Give it to her Mr Dan.' Two of her men trained their shotguns on me.

'No I don't think so. If I hand this over the NWO will be in total force within two years. If it had got to China the NWO would have been kept in check indefinitely. Also, so many poor souls, including JFK, have died for it and lastly I promised Guy Freeman, an old American gentleman, that I'd see it reach the right hands where it would do the most good for the people of the USA and Europe.'

'Don't be insane Mr Dan. It will be a bloodbath, we will all be killed.'

'Yeah right Zian, but when those shotgun shells hit me the folder will, like me, be shot so full of holes it will be of no use to anyone.'

Jia-Li, raising her voice in anger said, 'You maniac, you die for American President who was dead 25 years before you were born and you not even American!' Then she swung her gun back towards Zian.

'You will see your friend killed before your eyes because of your insane stubbornness. Then you will be killed.' I looked at Zian but didn't see a mysterious Chinese Secret Service man. I saw my pal the poem quoting rickshaw driver.

Then after a long pause I said, 'OK Jia-Li, I don't have that many friends so can't afford to lose him.' I took the folder out of my coat and threw it in her direction; one of her men sprang forward and grabbed it. I wondered if she would now kill us but if she did there would still be Winston & Co. to deal with. So, thinking clearly, she and her men backed off, keeping their guns trained on us, got in the Ram and sped off.

'You strange, remarkable man Mr Dan.'

'That's good coming from you Zian.'

'I very sorry for her', he said quietly. 'She now on way to American embassy. They made highest offer for NWO papers; 50 million US dollars. She spend too long in London, become too westernised, become obsessed with money. She lose touch with her ancestors.'

'For 50 million Zian I could lose touch with a whole crowd of people.'

'When Americans realise she has only a poor photocopy, not the original for sale, she will not leave embassy alive, nor will her bodyguards.'

'What are you saying Zian?'

'I am saying this is original copy.' He pulled back his coat showing the large folder. 'Jia-Li has the copy I made back at Winston's house. I took gamble on you being born in year of Dragon; brave but soft hearted remember? And also on our strong friendship.

Mr Dan, *There is nothing in the World like friendship, it is cleaner than love and older. It gives more and takes less, It is fine in the enjoying. In love all laughter ends with an ache. But laughter is the very essence of friendship.* Before you ask Mr Dan, that by Rupert Brooke, English poet. He die in First World War along with 20 million others organised and financed by international bankers, same as Second World War, where even more died and all wars since.'

'Zian, you've made one quote too far this time, I'm a fan of Brooke's work, I have all his poems back at the flat and that ain't one!'

'Dragon people jump to wrong conclusions, I did not say it was poem. That was excerpt from letter Brooke wrote to friend from Fiji in 1913.

'Why the hell didn't I let Jia-Li shoot when I had the chance?' I quipped. He began to laugh more than I'd ever seen him do before. The sailors on the motor launch shouted something.

'They say if I don't go now we miss rendezvous with freighter because tide is turning.'

'Let's hope World events turn for the better once you get that folder home.'

'It will, I promise.'

'Goodbye my friend.'

'Mr Dan, your ancestors are proud of you.' With that he ran into the sea, the water swirling around his legs. The sailors hauled him on board and with a roar of what sounded like high powered twin Volvo diesels the boat backed up fast, turned and sped out to sea, leaving a wide path of white foam on the surface. He stood in the stern with arm raised in a salute and called; 'My home in Shanghai is yours Mr Dan.'

Back in the Hummer once more Winston handed me an envelope saying 'Your pal asked me to give you this once he was on that boat out of here.'

Inside I found a small book; *The Sayings of Confucius* and a cheque for five grand. A note in Zian's handwriting said; *This will tide you over for while and maybe help you get another car. Your friend, Zian.* I felt choked with emotion, you bet it will tide me over, it'll keep me afloat for weeks, thanks pal.

Chapter 17 – A Letter To The President

In less than two hours we pulled up outside my place and Winston made me promise to come down to Brixton real soon. I did promise but knew it was one I'd probably never keep.

As I got out one of his men said, 'Looks like your neighbours is throwing a party.' I looked up and saw the floor below mine had the windows open, the lights were on, music was playing and people were laughing and shouting. As I climbed the rickety stairs a crowd of party goers came rushing out of the flat. I stood back against the wall to let them pass, the air was heavy with the smell of cannabis. Leaning by the door was a hard looking blonde girl of about 19 wearing large hoop shaped ear rings. She looked like she'd known many of those moments when women rule supreme.

'Hi I'm Lauren, you're Dan? I've seen you fight on TV.'

'Yeah, don't tell me I got badly beaten in my last fight.' She laughed.

'The party's breaking early but come in, have a drink.'

Early, I thought, it was nearly 5am! 'Another time Lauren, I've had a hell of a day.'

'Hey I've got a small packet for you.' She reached behind the door and handed it to me. 'An old guy; tall, thin, snappy dresser left it for you.'

'That'll be Bob my boss, thanks.'

As I carried on up the stairs she called, 'If we're too noisy just bang on the ceiling.'

As I opened my door the heat hit me. I'd left the central heating on but thanks to Zian I can pay the bill no problem. I took a shower, went to pour a whisky but changed my mind, from now on I'm cutting down on the booze, made a tea and before crashing out on my bed I checked my emails. I deleted all the junk before noticing one from Maria Moretti:

Hi Dan, you must be making waves over there. I was taken in for questioning by the Feds. They somehow knew I'd spoken to you, I told them sweet FA and my lawyer sprung me after two days.

Hope this is in time for your book. I have a contact who is big time in TV over here. The government have got cosy with movie star Tom Hanks who rewrites American history when he makes a movie. He recently made a TV series called "The Pacific" where we are portrayed as murdering devils and the Japanese are all angels during the Pacific War of the 1940s. And of course he made "The

Da Vinci Code"; anti-Catholic and anti-Christian. So he's the right guy for the job. They will secretly provide the mega bucks but he has to come up with a major ten part (Yes Dan, ten part) TV series ready for 2013, the 50th anniversary of JFK's murder. They've told him it must punch home to all those who are under fifty that it was Lee Harvey Oswald who killed JFK and no one else was involved, he acted entirely alone. One of our comedians said he's going to bring out a follow up series called "If You Believe That You'll Believe Anything". Just shows they're determined to stick to the party line and they will keep ramming it down our throats until the public accept it.

And before long if they don't they'll be arrested! What the hell Dan are they afraid of? Send me a copy when it's published. Take Care. Maria. X X

I sent a quick reply thanking her and saying how it may not be too late to include the information in the book as the proof copy had just arrived. I told her I'll make sure she gets a copy. I went on to say:

It's unbelievable that the White House is willing to go to such lengths even now to suppress the truth about JFK. And you can bet the USA along with the UK and some other powers are working out how to suppress the Internet as well.

Now Maria, I have incredible news. I got hold of Dorothy's original folder. I will call you tonight via the webcam and give you the full fantastic story. No I'm not kidding, in fact I have never been more serious in my life. Speak to you soon. Dan XX.

My mind then turned to Bob's packet, with trembling hands I opened it. I knew of course what it was. And there it was, my book! It had the words *Proof Copy* stamped across the front cover. A note from Bob read; *Dan, read this carefully word for word then read it again. Monday morning phone the office. Steve my head proof reader will have it up on the screen and you can go through it word for word. When it's perfect it will go to the printers. Call in later in the week, I want to discuss your next book.* Next book! Wow I'm on my way.

I hope this next one Bob, I thought aloud, *is something real tame like 'Stamp collecting for the over 60's'.* I looked at the cover, the pictures, and read a paragraph here, another there, but was too tired and excited to read it through. I'll do that in the morning. As I lay there drinking my tea in the soft light of my bedside lamp, various faces came into my mind's eye: Barney, Seb, Guy, Jock. I thought about the three assassins whose faces

I never saw and the fourth one, Anita, who tried to kill me in this very room. Then for some unknown reason I decided to do something crazy, but something I felt I must do. I went over to my desk and started a handwritten letter to President Obama. If Della were here she'd fall about laughing. OK, so he will never see it, let alone read it, but I'll feel better for writing it.

Dear Mr President,

Now that you are the President you will have been made aware of a whole range of information that other people would have no knowledge of. You almost certainly now know how and why the 35th President (John F Kennedy) was murdered back in '63. I beg you to go public and tell the people not only of America but the World the truth. Don't hide behind that rubbish about the "JFK Files will be released in 2017". Release them now today!

A recent poll of 15,000 Americans showed that 83% think that there was a conspiracy involved in his death. That means that 83% know they have been lied to, and therefore no longer trust their own Government. Since 1963 the USA has lived a lie. The most famous man on earth at that time was shot to death in broad daylight in front of the whole World, yet no one was ever brought to justice.

It must rank as the strangest crime in history. Forget Democrats and Republicans, this is bigger than politics. Be the first President to stand up and tell the truth. Those who killed him are almost certainly dead themselves by now. Or maybe you dare not offend the organisation that killed him because it still exists? If you were shot down today, do you think in nearly 50 years time someone would be writing this sort of letter to the White House?

Come clean, clear the decks, let the USA start afresh. Let's have the truth no matter how awful. Then a great American can rest easy in his grave after almost 50 years of strange deaths, murders, lies, deceit, cover ups and pure evil! Put an end to this long running curse on America. It will never go away as long as people like me care and want a truthful answer.

Take a look at that movie, see his head explode as the bullets hit him. I don't know or care if he was a good President. He was a human being. No way did he deserve that. You owe him and a couple of hundred million nobodies like me the truth. He was the 35th President, you're the 44th so that's eight who have done nothing to right this terrible wrong. Be the one who unlocks the truth and lets it fly free. And for that alone you'll be remembered as a great President.

Sincerely, Dan McQuade (London, England)

P.S.   Of course Mr President, when you give the order that the World must now know the truth about the JFK assassination, if someone has the authority to say 'no Mr President, we will not allow you to do that' then that reduces you to what my Chinese pal calls 'Just another cardboard cut-out'. Think about it....

I put the letter in an airmail envelope, stamped it and put it on the shelf. I'll post that in the morning; somehow it will make me feel real good. I was about to lay back on my bed when I heard a tap, tap, tap sound. I listened. There was no noise from downstairs; the party had broken up so what the hell is it. There it was again, sounded like someone wearing a large ring was tapping on the French windows. I took my gun out of the drawer, went over and pulled the blind an inch away from the wall.

The dawn was just breaking. The first rays of daylight were hitting my small balcony. There was no one there. Maybe the ghost of Anita Harga was coming back to haunt me. I slowly opened the door and there to my utter amazement sitting on the railing was Mickey.

'Hello Dan' he croaked weakly.

'Good God almighty Mickey!! I can't believe it's you.' He hopped or rather scrambled onto my forearm. He looked forlorn and bedraggled. I stroked his head and could see he was down to half his usual bodyweight, his once colourful plumage now dirty and dull. I took him through to the kitchen where he had a long drink of cold running water from the tap. Then talking to him all the time, I filled his dish with all his favourite nuts and seeds.

'I'll call in the vet tomorrow Mickey to give you the once over. Man I'm glad you're back, you wicked old bird. I warned you it was a jungle out there. I know you were born in one but that one out there is by far the most dangerous.' He looked at me as though to say *from now on I stay with you.* Tell you one thing Mickey, I think I've slowed down the advance of the New World Order. JFK would be pleased maybe at long last he, along with his brother and son, can rest easy. As Della would say, *not bad for a broken down cage fighter.*

'Tell you another thing Mickey, we must both be survivors and survivors understand one another right? Go on you can have the last word.'

With that he squawked a weak 'Hello Dan' and climbed wearily into his cage for a badly needed night's sleep.

Just then came another tap, tap. This time it was the front door. 'Who's there?' I shouted.

'Hi Dan, it's Lauren from downstairs, remember?' I opened the door slowly. She was leaning seductively with her head against the door frame, wearing one of those short bath robe things.

'Don't tell me you want to borrow some tea or sugar?'

'No, I heard you moving around and thought poor Dan, can't sleep either.'

'At this time of day most people are waking up not thinking about sleeping' I said thinking how stupid I sounded.

'Yeah well, I just thought we could get to know each other.'

With that she gave a sexy glance down at the bottle of Sherry she was holding. Looking at her more closely this time, I realised that under that rough expression she was quite pretty. Weak willed slob that I am, I heard myself say;

'A couple of Sherries and I'm anybody's. Sure, come in.'

She laughed, and the first thing she noticed was Mickey; 'Oh, you have a Macaw?'

'Yeah, you like parrots?'

'I love them, when I was a kid we had an African Grey.' Then she saw the book lying on the bed.

'Hey is this you, it says Dan McQuade?'

'Yeah, I'm trying not to be a fighter and be a writer instead, you don't get kicked and punched so much, but you do get shot at.' Thinking I was joking she laughed again. 'What's it about, what does JFK stand for?'

I thought; *this could only happen to me*. When I came back from the kitchen with the Sherry glasses she had also noticed the letter.

You're writing to that Obama guy who runs America, you know him?' She almost yelled.

'Yeah, we go back a long way.'

'Wow! He's real cool, I saw him on TV dancing with his wife, he's a mover.'

'Anyway, I'm not at all sure he does run America, I think International bankers do.'

'Who are they?' She asked, her big blue eyes looking at me with a puzzled expression.

'That's the million dollar question.' I replied more to myself than to her. She lay back on the bed drinking her Sherry, then slipping off her robe she climbed into my bed saying; 'Anyway, don't worry about all that now, come on Dan let's really get to know each other.'

As there was just no answer to that I got into bed with her, but before I did I put the cover over Mickey's cage. There are some things even wild, dangerous, aggressive Macaws from the South American rainforests should not be allowed to see.